Defying
Pack Law

Pack #1

Eve Langlais

New York Times Bestselling Author

Copyright © May 2011, Eve Langlais
Copyright © 2nd Edition April 2016
2nd Edition Cover art © Mina Carter, March 2016
2nd Edition Edits by Devin Govaere

Produced in Canada
Published by Eve Langlais
1606 Main Street, PO Box 151
Stittsville, Ontario, Canada, K2S1A3
http://www.EveLanglais.com

ISBN-13: 978-1533607744
ISBN-10: 1533607745

Chapter One

She ran full out. Her heart pumped wildly, and her breath came in harsh pants as adrenaline coursed through her body. The rush gave her muscles the extra oomph needed for a speed boost. She raced as if her life depended on it, her paws landing fleetly on the rocks she'd memorized. It would take only a small misstep to enter a world of pain because the area was peppered with dangerous foxholes, not all of them natural. She ghosted through the woods on paths marked only in the map of her mind, a labyrinth for the uninitiated. She practiced her escape route with single-minded intensity because, one day, her life might depend on it.

Hours later, physically exhausted, she returned to her home, which bordered the protected forest that spanned thousands of acres in this lost and godforsaken part of the planet, and shifted back to her human form. She strode, naked and proud, to her rear porch, secure in the knowledge that the only eyes watching her belonged to the simpleminded creatures of the forest. A rumble in the sky preceded the hovering storm and the cleansing rain that would wash the traces of her mad flight, keeping her secret routes safe.

She knew with an instinct borne of survival that the time fast approached when she would be forced to leave this haven of peace. Staying too long in one place was never a good idea, no matter the precautions she took. While currently Lycan free, the town and its location were too tempting to remain taint free forever. And when that happened, she'd move on, hopefully before she had to kill again.

It wasn't the life she'd dreamed of as a little girl, but at least it was hers.

There were times, when she fought off an unwanted werewolf suitor or fled yet another temporary home, that she wondered if she might not have been better off staying and accepting what fate held in store for her. Marrying the boy she'd once loved, whom her father—the most stern of her fathers—had approved of and whom, in her foolish youth, she'd given herself to. Accepting the fact that he'd share her body with others because pack law deemed he must. If she could only have believed him when he said it wouldn't be so bad.

Liar.

Immaturity didn't equate stupidity. She'd known, even in her infatuation, that he'd made a promise he couldn't keep. She'd seen it before in their little society, hidden amidst the human one. She had too much self-respect to want the life of chattel, passed around with her husband's permission to other males in the pack all because theirs was a society that bred males almost six to one. She'd watched the few women she'd known enter such marriages, only to see in some the light of love fade from their eyes as they were treated little better than vessels for birthing babes and sating the lusts of multiple mates. *Like my mother,* her poor, sad mother. No, she couldn't imagine a life like that.

Better to run than live as a slave, even if her dreams of the boy she'd left behind still haunted her, waking even after all this time sweaty and aching.

She shook her mane of hair in a bid to chase the melancholic memories and regrets that had no place in her current life—*the life I chose.*

Dana dressed in the robe she kept by the back door and then locked the place up. She set the alarm and checked her laptop for perimeter breaches, even though her own scrutiny while in wolf form had detected nothing. Everything appeared quiet, which seemed at odds with her jumpy nerves.

Paranoia at bay for the moment—but never far from her mind—she showered and went to bed.

* * * *

She ran, legs pumping madly, matching her breath coming in short pants. The crackling noise of her passage echoed through the sun-dappled branches, but she dared not slow. The one who chased her left no sound of his passage, but even though he moved as quietly as a wraith, the birds fell silent as they sensed the predator come amongst them. Her meandering flight brought her to a sun-filled clearing. Her chest heaving, she twirled, seeking him in the shadows. But as always, he snuck up on her. Arms, growing solid with brawn, wrapped around her and lifted her from the ground.

"Caught you," he whispered in her ear.

She squealed. "Nathan! Put me down."

"I will for a kiss."

She pretended to think about it and squeaked as he squeezed her tight. "All right, all right." She laughed. "You win. One kiss."

He turned her in his arms and looked down at her with those beautiful blue eyes. She could see mirth dancing in their depths. It went well with the crooked smile on his face, the one she wanted to kiss senseless.

She pursed her lips and tilted her head, all the invitation he needed to touch his mouth to hers. Oh, how she loved the electric current that ran through her when he held and embraced her like this. It made her whole body thrum and ache in the most intimate of places.

It was made even hotter by the fact that it was forbidden.

When his hands grew bold, tracing the contour of her buttocks, she pushed away from him. With a *mischievous grin, she took off running again. And, with his laughter surrounding her, he gave chase.*

Her alarm clock rang shrilly, jolting her from the dream. At least it had been one of the nicer ones, from a time when she still innocently thought things could turn out differently for her. *I used to be so oblivious.*

A hot cup of coffee—extra strong and bitter enough to make her grimace—further dispelled the foolish remembrance of her youth. She gulped down a bowl of Cheerios before she dressed in well-worn jeans, a faded plaid shirt, and steel-toed boots. Practical attire for her job at the lumber mill, a dirty, muscle-straining job but one that helped her stay strong, not to mention it also paid the bills.

It served another purpose as well. The mill, being the only place of real employment in town, meant she could easily keep track of the transients who came to work and ascertain their species—Lycan or human. When it came to the former, she took no chances. Run or die.

So far, she'd managed to fly under the radar of any packs in the environs and live peacefully. She'd stayed here long enough to even grudgingly come to like the mill and the people she worked with there. The idea of starting all over again didn't please her. Not only did the constant fresh starts get wearying, she was tired of constantly having to prove her worth. She'd worked hard to get to her current position of leader in the headsaw division. Only the best of the best could do it. Unlike the bull-chain operators, who simply pulled the logs into the mills, or the barkers, who ran the stripping machines, she needed skill. Not that she couldn't do their jobs. She could take over any position in the place, including that of the deck workers who rolled the logs onto the platform or the block setters who placed the logs into position. But any idiot with a little muscle could do those jobs. As leader of the headsaw crew, she was the one they counted on. She made sure they got as much high-grade lumber as possible from each log. It required precision and an ability to *feel* the wood, something she had a knack for.

In the beginning, she'd had to prove herself to the other workers in the male-dominated field. Many had scoffed at her when she'd shown up and applied with confidence. Used to mockery, she'd bet the doubters a round of drinks she could do it, and won, of course, to their chagrin.

It didn't end the pissing contests, but she'd gotten the job and grudging respect. Employed, she'd rented a house on the edge of the immense forest reserve and lived a careful life. One free of pack politics and emotional turmoil. A lonely existence empty of family and a partner. But better to live on her terms than as a sex slave to numerous men, which was what awaited her should she run across a Lycan who got past her defenses. She enjoyed a fragile freedom that required constant guarding.

Not trusting just her animal instinct to protect her, she'd splurged and set up a simple perimeter alarm. Anything bigger than a cat and the alarm went off, sending a signal to her laptop, which was always on and which, in turn, would alert her via cell phone. *How can I be lonely when paranoia is my constant companion?* she thought wryly.

She drove to work in her beat-up truck. Old, noisy, and a pig on gas, it served the purpose of getting her back and forth to work, and she wouldn't cry if she had to leave it behind, a lesson learned in one of her previous temporary homes, where she'd had to ditch her lovingly restored Mustang. *But I don't need objects to make me happy,* she told herself, even as she still regretted the loss.

She parked in the muddy parking lot and squelched her way into the building. The stench of the mill this close to the source was almost eye-watering, but she'd had plenty of time to get used to it. She dumped her lunch in the humming fridge and mumbled some good-mornings to the crews already there sipping coffee from their travel mugs. She snagged her time card and punched in. Grabbing a Styrofoam cup, she poured some of the sludge that passed as coffee.

"Why the hell aren't you lazy bastards already working?" she demanded.

"Line's down," Big Mike announced.

Stupid malfunctioning equipment. A delay like this would mean they'd have to work twice as hard to make up for lost time. "Again?" She rolled her eyes. "When is fucking management gonna get its head out of its ass and fix the damned belt with something other than spit and prayers?"

"When shit's worth gold," another of her crew answered.

She laughed as she nudged Mike to move over on the picnic table management had brought indoors for their use since chairs didn't seem to last. "Move over, fat ass," she ordered.

Big Mike chuckled as he slid over to make her some room. "Honey, my ass might be fat, but my cock is even wider." Mike held his hands apart two feet, and Dana grinned as she shook her head.

Dana didn't take offense. Working with men, she needed to have a laxer attitude, and getting up on her high horse over companionable ribbing would shut her out quicker than tattle-telling to the boss. "Damn, Mike. You are just too much man for little ol' me."

Laughter filled the room as they continued to banter back and forth.

Cory, a deck worker, stuck his head

inside the employee break room. "Hey, Dana. The boss wants to see ya."

"Now what?" she grumbled as she stood up and tossed her half-drunk coffee in the battered garbage bin.

"Tell him I got a hot date tonight and we can't work late," Mike called after her as she left to meet with her boss.

She walked into her foreman's office, expecting another speech on how the owners needed them to up production—*blah blah, blah*. In other words, the usual spiel he gave after every quarterly accounting. But it seemed complacency was to be her enemy today because she walked in and froze at the sudden, unmistakable scent of wolf.

Fuck. The kid in the office, the only name she had for the fresh-faced youth standing there, turned to face her, and his eyes widened. He opened his mouth, probably to say something stupid, and she gave him a cold glare to shut him up. He obeyed, but she didn't miss the interest lighting his expression.

A pity she'd have to douse that spark of life.

She only half listened to her boss as he asked her to show the kid around and find a spot for him to work. His regular training lackey was out sick, and given the log crews were behind due to machinery malfunctions, the annoying task of training fell to her.

The pup barely waited until they'd left the office to announce his intention. "I claim you."

"Not likely," she snorted.

"You can't do that. You're unmarked, making you free game to the first male who claims you. Pack law says so."

Dana whirled and, in a flash, pinned the annoying pup against the wall with a forearm across his throat. "Listen here, little boy. I don't want to be claimed and really don't give a shit what pack law says. In case you hadn't noticed, I chose to live outside of one. If you want to live, I'd suggest you forget about trying to claim me. I've taken down much bigger wolves than you."

The pup's face went slack with astonishment—only for a moment. Then male arrogance—also known as the dumbass syndrome—once again took over. "You can't threaten me like that, and you don't get to decide what you want. Pack law says I can claim any unmarked female."

Dana's patience snapped, and any squeamish feelings over what she had to do evaporated with his stance. "Really? Is that your final answer? Because, just so you know, my law says any prick who tries to claim me against my will either loses his dick or dies. So, what's your choice, puppy, because I'm losing patience really fucking fast."

When he would have opened his

annoying mouth again to spout some more nonsense, she kneed him. Where words tended to not work when a male was thinking with his cock, a dirty shot tended to wake them up real quick—that and she got sadistic pleasure out of seeing them gasp for air and turn all kinds of shades of purple.

She sauntered away, noting with her keen senses that he followed, if unhappily. He said not one more word to her as she went through the motions of showing him around. She didn't care if he retained anything or not. He wouldn't live to see the morning.

Her decision to take him out didn't please her, but she knew his type. She'd dealt with them before. Only one thing stopped them once they scented her—death.

Something alerted her coworkers to her simmering anger, probably her tight jaw and flashing eyes, because the regular crews refrained from saying anything to her face about her little shadow. It didn't stop them, though, from snickering behind her back when they thought she couldn't hear—wolves, even in human form, had much keener senses, including enhanced auditory ones. The mill workers joked about how she'd whip the new boy into shape. If they only knew.

She clocked out at five o'clock but got hung up by one of the guys, who grabbed her by the arm and teased her about her unwilling trainee. By the time she managed to extricate herself, the young wolf was gone.

"Fuck, fuck, and fuck again." She muttered expletives under her breath as she stalked to her beaten-up truck. She scanned the parking lot, more a mud pit with various pieces of rusted crap sitting on tires. She didn't find the pup. Hell, he could have been sitting right under her nose, but given she didn't even know what he drove, and the overpowering stench from the mill, she couldn't even track him. However, there were only two places in town to rent rooms, the majority of which were held by mill workers. She didn't figure he'd be hard to find. Unless he'd smartly left town.

Two hours later, after scouring the small town several times over, including the diner, bar, and pharmacy, she gave up. The pup seemed to have disappeared, taking the news of her existence with him. She drove home in simmering silence. She wanted to believe he'd left, moved on to greener and easier pastures. Her gut, however, said he'd be back, and she'd bet he was the type to bring friends.

Pulling into her drive, she hit the gas too hard and spit up gravel with her spinning tires. Not that she cared if she left a rut. The next owner could take care of it. It was time to move on. Dana slammed out of her truck and stalked into her house.

Un-fucking-believable. Forced to leave

because of a wet-behind-the-ears pup. Cursing and rigid with alert tension, she first checked her laptop for any signs of a perimeter breach. None of the alarms had been tripped—yet. She began throwing clothes into a duffel bag, a plan abandoned as the rumble of engines approached. She took a quick peek out her window and saw them coming up her drive. One vehicle, two . . .

Dana dropped her duffel bag and ran for the back door. She flew outside, tearing at her clothes as she sprinted across her back lawn.

She smelled the wolves before she saw them. Her eyes flicked from side to side, scanning her yard. She discovered a pair of them flanking the rear of the house. She vaguely wondered how they'd evaded setting off her sensors but didn't ponder it for long. One thought took precedence at this point—survival. It didn't take a genius to figure out that they'd planned to either flush her out into their waiting, furry net or, at the very least, corral her in a noose of werewolves, hoping numbers would take her down.

Like hell. She shifted while running, a feat that had taken practice, given the pain and distraction of exchanging one body for another. But her self-inflicted lessons served her well, as the approaching wolves faltered in surprise. She didn't waste the moment. She took off like a bat out of hell, following the escape route that existed purely in her mind, one ripe with pitfalls for the unwary.

She hit the shadows offered by the towering trees, the sound of pursuit hot on her heels. But she'd planned for this. She veered sharply to the left and gauged her footfalls to avoid the innocuous pile of leaves. She cleared the trap she'd set and sent up a quick prayer.

A yelp sounded from behind her, and she would have grinned had she not been intent on her getaway. One down, God only knew how many more to go.

The summer sun, close to setting, colored the woods a panoply of colors, but she was more interested in the increasing murk. She turned sharply again, moving in a zigzag pattern that brought her to a small stream, and while she hated the noise of her passage, she knew that this liquid trail would throw them off for a bit.

On and on she ran, her sides heaving, her tongue lolling, weaving in and out of the forest she'd grown to know. She avoided the trenches, snares, and holes she'd dug in her preparation for this day, all the while cursing the males who'd forced her to run. *Why does the word 'no' just not exist in their vocabulary? More importantly, why couldn't I have been born human?*

Wishing, though, did nothing to change her fate. She could rely only on herself and her will to survive—oh, and the nasty booby traps she'd laid. She wasn't going down without a fight. Occasionally she would hear a howl or a yelp as one of her pursuers met some of her hidden treats, but she didn't dare slow. Her gut screamed, *Danger*, and urged her to keep going.

Night fell, and she still kept moving, her gait slowing as the adrenaline began to wear off. She'd put miles between herself and the house she'd abandoned. Not far enough. Needing to rehydrate herself, she stopped for a quick drink and listened for sounds of pursuit.

The night surrounded her in an eerie quiet. Even the insects kept their silence. Dana didn't like it one bit. She took off again, slower, as she decided to forgo speed in favor of stealth.

She kept inhaling deeply, her nose sorting the many distracting scents. Nothing untoward appeared, and yet, something didn't seem right. The air hung too still. The forest seemed to hold its breath in an unnatural silence.

As she trotted across a circular clearing, bordered by towering trees, the sense of wrongness amplified, but before she could backtrack into the shadows, bodies fell from the trees and landed with thumps all around her.

Dana danced in place, her mind screaming at her for stupidly walking into a well-laid ambush. The naked men of varying sizes closed in on her, strangers all except for one, young pup. *That little bastard. He'll be the first to die.*

She lunged at the youth who'd betrayed her, barely noticing his eyes widening in shock before she caught his throat in her teeth. He didn't have time to shift—he died that quickly, with his blood spurting hotly and enticingly in her mouth. Her human side recoiled from the pleasure of the kill, but with her beast in control, she couldn't prevent the elation and thrill. She didn't rejoice long.

Heavy, furry bodies slammed into her, tearing her from their dead pack mate.

Dana fought for her life, snapping her teeth and ripping at any flesh she could clamp her jaw around. Not that it mattered. They were careful not to kill her, but their sheer numbers and strength battered her. Blow after ringing blow hit her. She staggered, determined not to give up. Human arms wrapped around her neck and cut off her air supply.

In a panic, she shifted, trying to use the defense moves she'd learned to unlock the chokehold—to no avail.

"Feisty little bitch. We're going to enjoy taking turns with you and beating out your defiance."

The speaker thrust himself against her backside, his sickening arousal evident. Dana thrashed, fear finally overcoming her courage, her scream of horror caught in her throat. More and more hands grabbed at her, and though she fought with all her strength, she couldn't escape.

They kept piling on top, copping painful feels and cracking a few ribs in the process. Body pinned to the ground, each lungful of air became sharp pain in her chest, and her dizziness grew.

"Enough!" their leader yelled. "We don't have time for this. We're not the only ones about this night. Don't worry. We'll all get a turn at her sweet cunt. Save your energy for when we get back to the house. You're gonna need it to win your spot in the hierarchy of who's gonna get to fuck the little bitch first."

Cheers erupted, which transitioned into howls, as the bastards cheered this announcement.

Dana moaned, unable to stop the creeping terror that enhanced the pain that threatened to drag her down in its grip. She feared blacking out and waking a victim of their perverted lust. She was yanked to her feet, her vision blurry but not enough to miss the leering faces all about her. Turned upside down and thrown roughly over a hairy shoulder, the excruciating agony against her abused ribs finally made her succumb to blackness. As her eyes lost focus and drifted shut, she couldn't stop one last panicked thought. *Please, don't let me wake.* She feared the nightmare to come if she did.

Chapter Two

Close, so fucking close. And once again, she'd outsmarted him and his pack. He should have placed more men at the rear of her house. He should have snuck up with them instead of coming to the front, hoping he could accomplish his task with words instead of force. He should have known better.

Did she hate him so much still? *Is she still so unwilling to forgive?* He'd had years to revise his stance, to get into a position of power where he made the rules, and changed them to suit his purpose.

The mad dash through the woods had cost him time and men. Even he had been forced to slow his chase because of her cleverness and ruthlessness in setting effective traps. She'd obviously prepared for this day, a fact that didn't hearten him. But it also wouldn't stop him. *Baby, when are you going to understand you are mine?*

He howled as he bounded into a clearing with a heavy stench of blood. The dark fluid soaked the ground, painting it black. The blood and the violence it implied didn't disturb him half as much as the scent he distinguished from the rest. *Her scent.*

He shifted back, uncaring of his nudity, and stood surveying the battlefield. Only one body remained, ignobly splayed. Everyone knew dead men, especially naked ones, told no tales, but their body could reveal much. He rolled the still warm form of the boy onto his back. The youth gazed straight ahead with glassy eyes. It left him impassive. He would have done worse had he caught him.

No one touches her. The mark he hunted stood out in glaring contrast to the rest of the dead youth's skin. The sign of the boy's pack, tattooed over his heart, was a map to the Lycans who'd dared take her. A symbol of a pack about to become extinct.

A more frightening question loomed in his mind—*do I have enough time to save her?*

Another wolf entered the clearing and shifted. Almost as tall as him but with a slimmer build, John held the position of best friend and beta. His solemn brown eyes took in the scene, and he shook his head. "Fuck. We just missed them."

"No fucking kidding, Sherlock," he growled. "Where's the rest of the pack?"

"They've got their trail and are following. Are you coming?" John asked.

"I'm heading back to the house and the trucks." He didn't need to waste time tracking, not when he knew the location of the pack that wore that particular brand. And what a surprise. They happened to be the rogue group the Lycan council had sent him to eliminate. Apparently, he should have taken care of them first before getting sidetracked by his personal business.

"Do you know who took her?"

"The rogues we were sent to wipe."

John grimaced. "Fuck. That doesn't bode well, you realize."

He just growled. Some things didn't bear mentioning aloud or even contemplating. "They'll be slowed down carrying her because I doubt she's gone willingly."

John regarded the dark forest pensively. "We'll let the ones tracking keep after them."

He caught the nuances of his friend's plan and approved. "If they're harrying at their heels, then they won't have time to stop and do anything to her. Come on then. We need to race back to the trucks so we can head to their den directly."

"So what's the plan once we get there?" his beta asked. He set his fingers to his mouth and loosed a sharp whistle followed by a series of short and long ones, a Morse code of sorts that would tell the wolves scattered in the woods where to head.

"We get her back." There was no hesitation. He had no choice.

His friend arched his brows in surprise.

"You do realize these are rogues?"

"I'll ask them first to give her back." A request he knew would be refused.

John scoffed. "Yeah, like that'll happen. What happens when they say no?"

His eyes turned cold and hard. "Then we start a war like the council requested, and we take her back anyway."

Chapter Three

Dana awoke. How unfortunate. And, boy, did she fucking hurt. The agony radiated from every part of her body so intensely it made her nauseous. It took her several moments to breathe past the pain.

She didn't move—it hurt too much—as she took stock of her situation, or what she could see from her prone position. It could be summed up in one word—bleak. Even in the near dark, she could see her cubicle of a prison: brick walls with crumbling mortar, a silver-inlaid door with a barred window that let in a fragment of light. The scent of death, comprised of sweat, blood, and tears, permeated the air, and she wondered how many others had found themselves in the same prison, gripped in the same despair.

The cement floor, cold and unforgiving, didn't make the most comfortable of pillows. But it was still preferable to what she imagined awaited her once they realized she'd regained consciousness. It took her a moment to realize the weight on her body wasn't fatigue and injury—great as they were—but chains. Silver chains. *How dangerous do they think me that they must pin me down in an obscene amount of silver?*

The heft of it proved onerous, but at least the burning pain of its poisonous touch managed to distract her from the rest of her body's damage, the cracked ribs being the most grievous and slowest to heal. Each inhalation threatened to drag her back into the darkness. Given time, her body would mend, a Lycan trait that usually served her well, but in this instance, it would mean a never-ending life of torture, or so she imagined, given what she'd seen of her captors so far. Her brief stint of consciousness in the packed truck had thankfully been short and yet long enough for the crude leader of the gang to tell her in gleeful detail the things he planned to do to her.

She attempted to stretch, the clanking of the metal almost stifling her scream of agony as the bruises she'd earned in her attempt to escape woke with a vengeance and made a lie of her earlier assertion the silver was more painful. She attempted to console herself with the fact that the throbbing agony of her body was a badge of honor proving she'd acquitted herself well against the brutes who'd hunted her down like the vilest of bitches. The remembered bellows of pain and the blood she'd made them shed made her grimace in a parody of a smile.

In the end, though, one female Lycan was no match for the strength of the dozen sent to capture her. *Bullies.*

All the bravery in the world also wouldn't stop what was to come because now the true nightmare would begin. The pain she endured at the moment would be nothing compared to the lifetime of humiliation and agony they planned to inflict. Female werewolves were rare. Rare enough that these males risked their lives to capture her. Rare enough that, even as they fought among themselves over who would claim her first, there was no question they would share her. Rare enough that she had no choice.

Frustration spilled over, and Dana screamed. The sound, loud and piercing, was filled with the despair and unfairness of the situation. She'd escaped from one life of gentle servitude, only to end up roped into a warped one, rife with violence.

Just wait until they try and bed me. I'll rip their fucking cocks off, she thought savagely. *I'll make them bleed and hurt.*

Her primal cry received a response in the form of thumping footsteps. The click of the tumblers in the lock preceded the ominous squeak of the silver-plated door being swung open. Dana narrowed her eyes at the man who stepped into her cell.

The pockmarked face of the prick who'd led the ambush leered down at her. "What's wrong, bitch? Feeling lonely? Eager for the taste of a man?" He grabbed his crotch in an obscene gesture that made her stomach turn. Dana didn't show her disgust, though. She wouldn't give him the pleasure. Instead, she spit in his direction.

"Pig. Only a coward needs to beat and tie up a woman to have her. Let me go and face me one-on-one, you chicken bastard. I'll show you how eager I am to see you." She grinned, a feral smile that didn't scare him—yet. He'd soon regret his choice in kidnapping her.

"Dirty-mouthed whore. I'll make you choke on your words." He unbuckled his belt, and Dana, still trapped by the silver, felt a frisson of fear dance up her spine. She didn't stand a chance trussed like a turkey. She'd hoped to goad him into releasing her and at least giving her a chance to fight—and die. But the coward had no intention of playing fair.

She stalled, for what she didn't know. *It's not like I've got anybody to come rescue me.* "How did you find me?"

Her abductor sneered. "One of my men stopped for lunch and came back saying he'd smelt pussy, the Lycan kind."

Dana wanted to kick herself. She'd assumed her mill stench covered her own when she came off work and stopped for a meal. "Fine, so you figured out I was there and sent your little spy. Doesn't explain how you knew where to find me in the woods."

"Our master told us," he hissed, his eyes lighting in a way that made her shiver.

"Master? You mean your alpha, don't you?" She didn't understand. She'd assumed this beast was the pack leader.

"I am alpha," he growled, thumping his chest. "The master just is and not to be talked about."

"So you're just a lackey?" she goaded in the hopes he'd lose his temper and end her before he did something worse.

Her comment dropped the miscreant to his knees, and he hauled her up by the chains, the pain so intense that she couldn't even squeak out a scream. She did, however, moan as her eyes rolled back in her head, but darkness refused to claim her.

His spittle sprayed her as he spoke with a tight voice. "Mouthy little bitch. I might be his servant, but because of the master, I'm more powerful than you can imagine. Now since you like working that mouth of yours so much, I'll give you something to choke on." He released her and she fell back on the floor, gasping as needles of agony radiated throughout her body.

The news that someone pulled this pervert's strings like a puppet didn't have the power to stun her like the image of the dirty pig unbuttoning his pants. He'd prepared to shove them down when the sounds of screams came to them.

With a frown, her pockmarked thug buttoned back up. "Fucking idiots. Now what the hell are they up to? Don't go anywhere, my feisty slut. I'll be right back to take care of you as soon as I knock a few heads together."

She'd hoped he would leave the door open in his distraction, but the door swung shut behind him with a clank. The sound of the key turning in the lock killed all hope of escape.

Dana closed her eyes and couldn't help the tear that leaked from the corner of an eye. *How did my life come to this? When did dying become a choice more preferable than life?* Even worse, in her current condition, she couldn't even be preemptive and take her life before the brute would return to take her body.

Misery engulfed her, and she shook on the cold floor, oblivious to anything but her pain, both physical and mental. *Stupid. Stupid. I should have never left my pack. At least there I had a chance for happiness. Maybe I would have been one of the lucky ones who didn't mind sharing my bed with more than one man. If I could turn back the clock, return to that time, I'd do things differently. I wouldn't rely on my emotions to guide my actions but take charge instead and make the situation one I could live with. Choose my fate instead of having someone else, someone who doesn't care for me, decide my future instead.*

But as her father used to say with a sneer, wishes didn't grow on trees, and all the recriminations in the world wouldn't change her current situation.

The noise outside battered through her despondency. She tried to block it out, knowing the savagery was somehow connected to her. Probably a rematch to decide who would get the first turn.

However, the strident screams—death knells—were impossible to ignore.

The chaos of violence moved closer, or so she judged by the increase in volume, until it appeared to have arrived right outside her cell door. She held her breath as she listened. The unmistakable sound of flesh striking flesh and heavy breathing drifted through the barred window in the door. With a thump and a gurgle, dead silence suddenly reigned.

Dana's stomach fluttered. *Rescue?* Could she finally be so lucky?

Bang! Bang!

Something heavy pounded at the door, denting it. *What the fuck?* Her eyes widened in disbelief. Solid steel did not dimple without tremendous force. *Tell that to whatever is doing it.* Something beat at the door, and bit by bit, incredible as it seemed, the silver barrier crumpled until seams appeared as the door separated from the frame. Fingers that ended in sharp claws curled around the edges, and with a groan and screech of bending metal, the door was torn off its hinges.

Dear sweet fucking lord. Dana almost wet

herself in fear.

A beast stood in the doorway, literally. Taller than the doorframe, he loomed, blocking out the light but not enough that she couldn't make out certain characteristics, such as the fact that he sprouted dark hair all over and sported pronounced canines and a muzzle. A wolf-man, or so it appeared, something she'd never seen or even heard of before. The beast moved closer, ducking to pass through the doorframe, and she pegged his height at close to seven feet. The hulking wolf-man snarled at the sight of her, and his yellow eyes flashed with ominous light.

He took a heavy step toward her, and Dana, usually so brave, couldn't help but whimper. The pathetic sound halted the creature in its tracks. Before her wide-eyed gaze, the wolfish features shrank in on themselves, melting and reshaping into the face of a man. A face she recognized, even though she hadn't seen it in over twelve years.

He shook his head at her. "Caught you," he announced in a low timbre that still had the ability to make her tummy flip over, even in her current state.

Her heart raced faster. Her past had finally caught up to her, and the shock of it, along with the rest of her injuries, thankfully made her black out.

Chapter Four

Nathan looked down at Dana's still form and seethed. Her naked flesh was covered in bruises, scratches, and welts. Even more astonishing, her captors had feared her enough to wrap her body in links upon burning links of silver. He dropped to his knees, and ignoring the sizzling pain, he grasped the silver chain and pulled it apart as easily as snapping thread. Her skin was chafed red and blistered where it had touched her, and he boiled with anger.

I'm going to kill them slowly and painfully. He'd reserve a painful punishment for the dirty miscreants—those who still lived, that was— who'd dared touch the woman he'd claimed as his when still only a boy. Never mind she'd run from him. Dana was, and always would be, his.

His beta appeared in the doorway and whistled as his keen gaze took in her state. "Holy fuck. What kind of sick bastards treat a woman like that?"

The kind who need to die twice. Nathan couldn't speak. He couldn't. Anger and grief over her condition choked him. He sniffed her, the stench of her pain and blood heavy enough to pull his wolf to the surface to growl at the insult done to his woman. But relief tinged his emotions, as he didn't find any traces of rape. *Thank God.* Healing her body would be easy given her lycanthrope blood.

Healing emotional trauma would have been a lot harder.

He scooped her up, her weight like nothing in his arms. He winced as her face spasmed into a grimace as he unwillingly caused her pain, but he had no choice. He couldn't leave her lying there for the amount of time she'd need to heal.

He cradled her to his chest, wishing he had a blanket to cover her as he strode past his beta, who had joined him in freeing Dana, along with several others from the pack.

John sucked in a breath as he got a closer look at her. "Damn. They beat the living crap out of her."

"Gee, I hadn't noticed," Nathan replied through gritted teeth. "Status report."

"Eleven of the bastards are dead, but the leader and several others got away. We saw evidence of others living here, women too, but they appear to be gone."

Nathan turned a cold gaze onto his beta. "I want the cowards found and brought back to me—alive. Especially the leader." He had plans for the bastard, painful plans.

"Eddie and Joe are already tracking

them."

"Good. Let's get her home." Nathan emerged from the cellar of the dwelling in which they'd found her imprisoned. In the light of the fires burning as his men set the makeshift compound alight, Dana appeared even frailer, her injuries more glaringly bright. Nathan breathed deep of the vengeance he'd wrought. The scent of carnage hung in the air, a miasma of violence that would serve as warning, hopefully, that his pack meant business. *Touch my woman, and face the consequences.*

It mattered not that he hadn't officially marked her or that she'd fled him so long ago. *She is mine.* How she'd managed to evade for so long not only him but also the scores of other Lycans hot on her trail was a mystery. Her scent shone like a bright beacon that drove him wild with an urge to possess her, to mark and claim her. *And claim you I will, willing or not. I won't let you leave me again.*

The growl of his Jeep as it approached made him hug her to him tighter. Kody was at the wheel, and with a flourish, he swung it into the gravel drive and leaned over to open the passenger door, flashing a white-toothed grin.

"I see you caught the runaway. Awesome." His smile faltered as he caught a glimpse of her. "What the fuck did they do to her?"

Nathan just growled.

John replied, "Apparently, they mistook her for a punching bag. Ignore Nathan. He's just bent 'cause she fainted when she saw him. Can't say as I blame her. That's one ugly-ass mug he's got."

If Nathan's cargo hadn't meant more than his pride, he'd have punched his best friend's lights out. As it was, he made a mental note to do so later.

Kody, usually the jovial one, didn't reply to the banter. It seemed he couldn't tear his green eyes from her unconscious form. "Is she going to be okay?"

"She will be," Nathan replied—*she has to be.*

John opened the rear passenger door and hopped in before holding out his arms to take Dana. Nathan just glared at him. No one would touch her until he'd made her irrevocably his. He wouldn't take any more chances.

John snorted. "You can't get in while holding her, man. You might end up hurting her more. She's not going anywhere, and I'm not going to steal her. Tell your beast to take a pill."

Nathan sighed. His rational side understood John was right, but he still found it hard to hand her over, even for the few seconds it took to clamber into the backseat and get her back. He didn't like the keen interest both his friends showed in her. Sharing Dana wasn't a part of his new plan, not knowing what he did about her.

Her face contorted for a moment in pain at the shuffle as they got situated, and Nathan's rage bubbled up all over again. *If only I'd caught up to her sooner, this would have never happened.* "Get the syringe," he barked.

"She's gonna be pissed if you dope her," John remarked as he leaned over the seat to grab the med kit in the back.

"She's going to be pissed no matter what once she wakes up. I'd rather that not happen until we've made it back to the compound." He left unsaid, *where running away will be a lot harder now since we beefed up security.*

John rummaged in the kit until he located the needle filled with a tranquilizer, a must for the times they needed to bring in a wild rogue for questioning or, in this case, a reluctant female.

"Go ahead." Nathan watched as John pricked her shoulder and depressed the plunger. At the sharp prick, Dana's eyes shot open, wild with anger and pain.

"You bastard," she spat. "I'm gonna-gonna..." Her voice trailed off as the heavy-duty tranq put her back to sleep, a deep one that she wouldn't wake from until he had her right where he wanted her—in his house and in his bed.

John handed him a blanket as Kody took off with spinning tires. Nathan tucked it around her as best he could, uncaring of his own nudity. John managed with some contorting to get into his tracksuit and waved Nathan's at him.

"Come on, man. Hand her back over for a second and get your bare ass covered. No one wants to see your dick. Besides, I want to get our deposit back on this baby from the rental place. I don't need your ass sweat stinking it up and costing us extra."

John's humor pulled a smile from Nathan, and he handed his precious burden over to his beta, only long enough to pull on his own clothing. He had to admit he did feel a little better clothed. He also took an extra moment to get his boots on. Dressed, he held out his arms, and John, with a wry smile at his impatience, handed Dana back. Nathan settled her into his arms and finally relaxed enough to look at her and past the bruises marring her skin.

She'd changed in the last twelve years, matured. She'd let her hair grow out, and it tumbled about her in a messy golden wave. Her skin, the parts unmarked by violence, was lightly tanned and just as soft as he remembered, he found, when he traced a finger across the curve of her cheek to lips still plump and full. She'd lost the softness of youth, just like he had, but he didn't mind the toned muscles he'd noticed in her arms or the flat ridges of her stomach. A life on the run spent in defense mode would make anyone hard. He'd soon see to it that she regained the soft life she deserved.

He stroked her hair with a gentleness his friends would look askance at. He'd been anything but gentle these last couple of years. He hadn't had a choice. With the Lycan population explosion across the country, and the increase in rogues, survival was for the fittest only. As pack alpha, he'd fought to get his position, fought his own father, as a matter of fact, who refused to face the fact that the world had changed and they needed to change with it. But that had been only the beginning of his battles. He'd invested time, sweat, and money into making their compound secure, in making life for his pack a better one.

Yet, in everything he'd done, he'd never forgotten his primary purpose—find Dana and make her his.

To have her so close to him again, even pissed off and injured, completed something in him. She represented the missing puzzle piece in his life, and he'd never let her go again. Even better, he'd do his best to make sure she never wanted to leave.

If she didn't kill him first.

* * * *

John watched Nathan cradling Dana's

injured body and fought the urge to take her from him. He'd heard of the animalistic need to possess unclaimed Lycan females. He'd actually laughed about it. As resident physician, he'd deemed himself above such a base need, even as he'd watched others succumb. After all, he'd met other unmated Lycan females, and while he'd felt at times a mild interest, he'd never experienced or expected anything like the magnetic pull Dana exuded.

His recollection of her from way back was vague. He'd left for university before she'd matured enough to be interesting. During his brief visits home, he'd heard about her from Nathan, and even more about her after she ran away. He'd puzzled about the girl who'd made his best friend fall into a funk after she left. He'd wondered what kind of golden pussy she had to make Nathan obsess about finding her again.

But now, faced with her and, even worse, after having touched her, he couldn't deny the draw. It didn't help that his wolf stirred restlessly in his mind and urged him to regress to a more primitive state, pushed him to want to shed his humanity and challenge his best friend and alpha over the right to claim the female. *Or,* as his mind slyly reminded him, as pack law permitted, *share her.*

Were he human, the thought of sharing a woman, any woman, with another man would have horrified him, sent him running. And the human part of him cultivated at their schools did recoil, but his Lycan side that had grown up in a polyamorous household didn't care. It wanted this woman no matter what. He'd heard the orgy stories from other mated groups, seen the movies. Hell, his own mother had shared her bed with all his fathers, sometimes at the same time—a mental image he blocked quickly. Group matings were a part of his heritage, and while he'd never actually thought he'd indulge, he no longer found himself so sure. *Who am I fucking kidding? I can't deny the idea of watching and participating in a group fuck doesn't have its appeal. Well, so long as the other guys keep their body parts to themselves.*

Of course, there were a few problems with his fantasy about sharing the golden she-wolf. One—Nathan had made it abundantly clear he'd never share, not after losing her all this time. And second, from what John had learned about Dana over the years from his friend's drunken ramblings, one of the reasons Dana had fled was to avoid being forced into a polygamous relationship. *I wonder if, maybe with the right incentive, she'd change her mind?*

Watching Nathan tenderly stroke her, seeing Kody's eyes in the rearview mirror tracking them, and inhaling more than likely her scent, John wanted to sigh. *Ah shit. Not him too. Talk about a clusterfuck in the making.*

The couple of hours' drive to the small airstrip was done in tense silence. Nathan had retreated into an uncommunicative shell. Dana slept, still drugged. Kody drove with one eye on the backseat. And John rubbed his temples, trying to dispel the headache caused by his clenched teeth.

Only once they stopped on the runway did Nathan snap out of it. "John, you're coming with me. Kody, you go back and meet up with the boys we left behind tracking. Even if they haven't found those bastards, get your asses out of there. There's something about this whole setup that stinks, and I'd rather have you back home protecting the compound than out here by yourselves. I'll send the plane right back for a pickup."

"Aye, aye, Captain," Kody replied with a grin and salute.

John hopped out of the truck and came around to take Dana from Nathan. Perhaps a little too eagerly judging by the dark glare his alpha shot him. John couldn't have cared less. Holding her again did strange things to him. There was arousal, which kind of shamed him given her battered state, but a surge of even stronger protectiveness swamped him, a desire to save her from harm. His wolf's need was more basic—mark the woman.

Not wanting to give her up too quickly, John strode away from Nathan, who gave last-minute instructions to Kody. John made his way to the plane. He moved gingerly up the rickety metal stairs, trying not to jostle Dana more than necessary, and went through the open door. The eight-seater plane wasn't quite as comfortable as the truck, nor were the seats spaced in a way he could sit without squishing Dana.

Not that he got to keep her for long. Nathan came pounding up the stairs with a growled, "Okay, asshole, hand her back."

John didn't argue, not with her injured and in the way. He handed her back and surveyed the seating dilemma.

"Do you think your buddy will care if I rearrange the seating?"

Nathan's eyes flicked over to the cramped seats and back. "If he has a problem, I'll handle it. Make some room."

John didn't have the same kind of brute muscle Nathan did, so he didn't bother trying to arm wrestle the offending seat out of the way. He took his boots to it—and didn't move the damned thing.

Nathan sighed. "Hold on to her again, and try not to cop a feel, would you?"

John happily obliged, snuggling her into him protectively while Nathan bent over and grabbed the offending seat and lifted it straight up and off the bracket that held it.

John frowned at him. "Why the hell

didn't you tell me I had to lift it instead of trying to wobble it?"

Nathan grinned. "And miss watching Mr. Cool look like an idiot for once?" Nathan seated himself in the seat behind the vacated one and, with plenty of room to stretch out his legs, held out his arms for Dana.

John gave her back and headed to the rear of the plane for their luggage and his more extensive medical kit. Armed with a stethoscope, among other things, he derived great pleasure in saying, "Peel the blanket off so I can get a look." And horrible as it might be given the situation, John didn't just mean her wounds either. *I'll probably burn in hell for ogling her naked body while she's passed out, but I never claimed to be a saint.*

* * * *

Nathan could see John's interest in Dana. He didn't like it one bit. There was a time long ago, before Dana had left, when he'd imagined John would be one of the men he'd share his future mate with as per pack law. But, now, having her back again, Nathan found himself less than keen with that idea, a fact that he'd share with Dana if she ever gave him a chance to say his piece.

Jealousy or not, though, he couldn't deny Dana needed the attention of a doctor. While her Lycan blood would heal her, broken bones still needed to be set straight, and while rare, there was still a chance of infection.

Nathan pulled back the blanket, exposing her upper chest and breasts that were more defined than he remembered. The cooler air of the cabin made them pucker, and his mouth dried up, even as lust shot through him, hardening his cock. A quick glance up caught John staring with his mouth open, his eyes glazed.

"Get on with it," Nathan growled.

John didn't reply, just went to work checking her heart rate, blood pressure, and other vitals. He then proceeded to gently clean the myriad scratches that covered her from head to toe. Nathan cursed himself all over again for not having arrived sooner. It killed him to see the pain she must have suffered.

Never again. I promise.

The exam done, John injected her with some antibiotics to prevent infection, along with another dose of tranquilizer. Exhausted, Nathan closed his eyes, memories of the past catching up, memories of Dana from a time before she hated him.

He'd noticed her from a young age, not that he let her or his buddies know. He did, after all, have a reputation as a tough-ass to retain.

When she'd finally gotten old enough,

he'd begun to court her in secret. He'd had no choice, even as she assumed their furtive meetings were because of her own stringent parents. The truth was it would have driven Nathan's father—a man who ensured through tests that Nathan was his—wild if he'd known. At the time, Dana wasn't considered good enough for the son of an alpha. But eventually Nathan had reached a point in his feelings that he didn't care. He loved and needed her.

Dana had drawn him with her smiles and laughter, with her tough inner core and the way she looked past his sometimes brutish nature. In fact, she'd told him on more than one occasion, with blushing cheeks, that she enjoyed it when he pulled the dominant male on her.

And he'd loved making her melt. Then the night he'd claimed her body, everything changed. He'd had lots of years to regret the fact that he hadn't marked her that fateful night. But he'd foolishly believed in pack law, and he'd lost her.

And now that I have her back, I won't make the same mistakes of the past.

Chapter Five

Dana knew she was caught in a dream, a recurring one, but she couldn't wake herself, and she was forced to watch and relive the pain of the most defining moment of her life.

"Marry me. Be my mate." Nathan dropped to a knee and gazed up at her with shining blue eyes. It awed her that this hunk, strongest of all the boys, wanted her.

She tousled his dark hair, unable to resist its thick waves. "Are you insane? I just graduated from high school and haven't even started college yet." She protested, but with a smile. Who could resist the romance of the moment, and who could resist Nathan? She'd loved him it seemed like forever.

"So what? You can still take classes as my wife. Why wait? You know we're meant to be together. To become mates for life."

His use of the word "mates" reminded her of one uncomfortable fact. "But I can't shift into a wolf like you, which means it won't be a true mating bond." Not to mention they couldn't have children because, like a human, dormant Lycans couldn't get pregnant from a shifter. Wolves could only mate with wolves if they wanted pure bred pups. The fact that Dana's beast remained dormant meant the only children Dana would ever enjoy would belong to other men, human men.

"I don't care if you're a dormant. Actually, it's kind of a blessing because that means I can keep you all to myself."

His words were an uncomfortable reminder of the society she belonged to, even flawed as she was. As a Lycan who couldn't make the transition to wolf, pack law didn't require that her mate share her with his pack brothers. She was considered no better than a human. Her defect meant they could belong exclusively to each other.

"Your father will never agree," she said softly.

Nathan's brows drew together. "I really don't give a fuck. You're the one I want, the one that makes my wolf howl. Once he sees ours is a true mating, he won't be able to refuse."

Dana wanted to believe him, but Nathan's father was scary, and not just because of his alpha status in the pack.

His hand clasped hers tightly, and she could read the uncertainty in his eyes as she hesitated. How could she let him doubt a moment longer her love for him? The only thing that mattered was their love for each other. Everything else would work out.

"Yes, I'll marry you," she cried, throwing herself at him. She hit his body, and they tumbled in the soft green grass, his body cushioning her fall. They wrestled as they embraced, the laughter of their youth music to accompany the setting of the sun.

When his touch became too bold, she pushed away from him, tempering her rejection with a smile. "Now that I've said yes, surely you can wait a little longer?" Strictly raised with a heavy-handed father, Dana had preserved her virginity, waiting for the one. Waiting for Nathan to realize she'd grown up.

"You're killing me," he groaned as he feigned stabbing himself with a dagger.

She giggled. "You are such a ham."

"I prefer the term 'dog,'" he replied with a leer.

She brushed his hair from his forehead. How she loved him. Almost nineteen and finally filling out his lanky frame, he was everything she could ask for in a mate, and even more amazing, he wanted her, flawed or not, too.

Why was she denying them both? Her body and desire burned as hotly as his. He'd chosen her above others, and she wanted no other man. She kissed him again, softly. He responded back with the same gentleness, and she made a bold decision. She pushed him down onto the soft grass and straddled him.

When he quirked a brow in question, she replied by tugging off her shirt. The immediate burning gaze he turned on her made her insides melt.

"Are you sure?" he asked, even as she could feel his erection pressing against the crotch of her pants.

She didn't reply, although she did blush when, with fumbling fingers, she unclasped her bra. But embarrassment over her bold action faded when his hands drew her down for kiss and he murmured, "You are so perfect."

He rolled them so that she lay beneath him. He tore his shirt in his impatience to remove it, but her giggles were stifled when he pressed his body against hers, skin to skin. Her nipples pebbled against his chest as his tongue explored her mouth. His enthusiasm proved contagious and her hands roamed over the smooth skin of his back, clutching at him tightly when he inserted a thigh between hers and pressed against her cleft. Even with the clothing separating those regions, it excited her.

She moaned against his mouth and clutched him tighter. He tore his lips from hers and scorched a trail down her neck, his hot mouth on her bare skin making her gasp then cry out as he caught her puckered nub in his mouth and sucked.

Dana arched against him, the electric sensation filling her with a warmth and longing she didn't understand—but wanted more of. He switched his mouth to her other breast while Dana writhed and moaned with pleasure.

His lips trailed lower, tickling over her soft belly and stopping at her waistband. She held her breath and opened languorous eyes to peer down at him. His blue eyes glowed, and his lips quirked as he used his teeth to unsnap her jeans then pull down the zipper. His hands tugged her pants down, leaving her clad in only her cotton briefs. Dana now wished she'd worn something sexier, not that he seemed to care if his burning gaze was an indication.

Nathan stood, and his hands went to his own zipper. Her cheeks flushed, and she closed her eyes but heard him as he stripped himself as well.

"Look at me, Dana."

She didn't want to, suddenly embarrassed. Nudity among Lycans was one thing, nudity for the sake of lovemaking a whole other.

He covered her body with his, the shocking heat from his rod pressing against the cloth of her panties. Startled, she opened her eyes and found him staring intently at her.

"Do you want me to stop?"

And disappoint him—disappoint herself? "M-make love to me," she replied, her trepidation fading at his possessive look.

His hand slid down her side to her hip. A

ripping sound and her panties were gone. She spread her thighs at his urging, and he settled his body between her legs. He bent down to kiss her, and she clasped at his shoulders, tensing at the probing of his cock. He pulled back and bent himself to suck at her nipples until he had her arching. As he laved her breasts, he slid a hand between their bodies and cupped her sex. She couldn't help the moisture that seeped at his gentle touch.

Her moist sex acted like an awaited signal because he braced himself above her again, the head of his shaft poking at her pussy. Then he pushed his way in.

Her breathing hitched at the stretching sensation. Slowly he inched into her until he met the barrier of her innocence. With a swift thrust, he swept past it.

The pain of her breaching made her cry out, but he remained gentle with her, letting her adjust around his size before moving again. The sensation was odd at first, but as he butted up against and in her while kissing her, her passion reignited, and soon she met him, thrust for thrust. She panted, her body building toward something, something that felt so good she keened and perspired. When her orgasm hit, a mind-boggling event that saw her crying out his name, she knew she'd made the right choice in letting him claim her body. She clasped him to her when he bellowed his own pleasure and collapsed on top of her.

"I love you," she whispered, overcome at what they'd shared.

He nuzzled her neck, placing soft kisses on her skin. "And I love you, baby. From now on, it's just going to be you and me, forever." She liked the sound of that.

He rolled them so he lay on the bottom, and they snuggled together in the aftermath, her body draped over his. Passion assuaged, she blushed to think of how she would dress again under his avid gaze. Her ardor now cooled, her shyness increased. She reddened against his smooth chest as she realized she'd have to stand up and clothe herself soon. They would both have to, for the sun had set and night fell, bathing the glen in shadow, which meant her father would be expecting her home.

Along with the brightening night stars, the moon arrived. The wispy cloud cover of earlier parted to reveal the white globe in its full majestic glory. Its appearance meant the pack would be gathering for its midnight run shortly. No Lycan could resist the call of a full moon. Heck, younglings past the first spurt of puberty tended to spontaneously shift.

Not a thing she worried with around Nathan. As a full Lycan, he'd long ago mastered the moon madness that affected their kind, a madness she'd never experienced as a dormant.

The moon's rays bathed her nude body,

turning her skin the color of alabaster. Dana squirmed as her exposed and illuminated skin first tickled then itched. She jumped up from her cuddly spot on Nathan, suddenly uncaring of her nudity as the itch turned into pain.

"What's wrong?" Nathan asked, concern etching his voice. He stood and reached his hands out to her.

Pain ripped through her, sending her muscles into involuntary spasms. "Nathan, help me," she gasped before falling to her knees, still convulsing.

His strong hands came to stroke her as she twisted on the ground, the searing pain spreading outward into all of her limbs.

"Oh my God, Dana. You're changing. You're finally changing." He sounded so excited, but caught in a screaming agony that seemed never-ending, she could only wail, and then howl, as her body morphed with sickening cracks into that of a wolf.

Dana panted as she lay on the ground, her body changed. Disoriented, but thankful the pain had receded, she struggled to her feet, wobbly like a newborn colt. She shook her head to clear a vision that, while sharper, no longer perceived things in a manner she was used to. Nathan's hands continued to stroke her fur.

"Dana, you're a wolf." He sounded so awed.

She, however, wasn't as impressed. It had

bloody hurt.

"It must have been the moon," he said in wonder.

Dana snorted, or tried to. What came out was more like a cross between a bark and a wheeze. Wolf mouths weren't meant to speak human words. But her mind still worked, and it churned furiously, trying to understand what had just happened.

She'd been exposed to the moon many a time before, mostly by her father, in an attempt to trigger the change. He'd tried in her tweens, when her menses first started. He'd tried in her teens, when she grew into her more womanly shape.

He'd even tried after feeding her one nasty concoction after another, all attempts to trigger her dormant Lycan gene. None of it had worked, so why now?

Dana's eyes caught the pile of clothes on the ground, and the gears in her mind stopped whirring. The only difference this time was the loss of her maidenhead to Nathan.

Dana wondered for a horrified moment if she'd be forced to confess her transgression with Nathan to her father. She hoped the fact that she could now shift would distract her father from asking the embarrassing question of how. And, even more important, prevent the beating he was sure to inflict for having given in to her baser desires.

But that worry could wait for later. She was a wolf!

She moved a few steps forward, the adjustment to four limbs strange but not hard to pick up. She heard Nathan gasp, and she turned too quickly, almost landing on her nose. Nathan was gone. In his place stood a dark-haired wolf that seemed to grin at her with its lolling tongue.

She gave him back a canine grin of her own. Suddenly, she didn't feel too bad anymore. The pain was gone. Her dad would probably be ecstatic, and best news of all, she was destined to become Nathan's wife. With a joyful yip, she walked then ran across the clearing into the woods, the exhilaration of her new body filling her.

She raced side by side with Nathan, encountering other wolves also out loping under the moon. Their howls filled the night sky, and Dana, caught up in the moment, enjoyed every second of it.

* * * *

She awoke late the next day, her father having let her sleep in and miss her chores given the incredible events of the night before. And she wasn't just talking about the fact that she could now shift like the others. Nathan had asked her to marry him! She would be his wife. As if thinking of him had conjured him, she heard a tapping at her window.

She flung back her covers and went to the window in only a T-shirt and underwear. Modesty seemed stupid given their lovemaking. Not to mention her sudden change back into human shape, in all its naked glory, to an audience of several. Her blushes had at least kept her hot until someone gave her a shirt to drape herself in. Even more warming were Nathan's glares at those who openly leered. Who said jealousy wasn't attractive?

She unlocked her window and slid it open so her fiancé—she giggled in her head at that title—could come in.

He grinned widely at her as he enveloped her in a hug that made her squeak. She squealed as he twirled her around. Then she got a look at his face.

"What happened to you?" she gasped.

Both of his eyes were swollen and purple, and his lips puffed up. She pushed back and tugged at his shirt. He didn't fight her as she lifted it and saw the bruises that peppered his skin. "Oh, Nathan," she wailed, her eyes filling with tears.

"I had a disagreement with my dad. Don't worry. It's already mostly healed."

She sucked in a breath, horrified that this was what he considered better. How badly had his dad hurt him and why? "But—"

He didn't let her finish her question,

kissing her breathless instead. "Forget about me. How do you feel?" he asked.

How like him to be more concerned about her. She moved back into the circle of his arms and leaned her head on his chest. "It feels like last night was a really weird but wonderful dream." One she'd treasure forever.

"It was real. Are you excited you've found your wolf?"

"I'm most excited by the fact I'm going to be your wife," she answered honestly, peering up at him as she twined her fingers through the hair that curled at his nape.

A shadow crossed his face. "Me too. You'll be glad to know we've actually got permission from both of our parents to go ahead. And don't worry, my dad and yours promised we'd have plenty of time between now and the first baby for us to enjoy each other."

Her brow creased with confusion. "Of course we will. Besides, silly, having a baby doesn't mean the fun stops. After all, we'll need to have lots of fun to make that big family we talked about." The mention of babies elated her. Now that she'd come into her heritage, she could have pups of her own instead of envying those around her.

His jaw tightened. "Of course we'll still have fun together. It'll just be an adjustment sharing you. I'd kind of gotten used to the idea of having you all to myself."

Dana froze and searched his face for a hint she'd misunderstood. "Excuse me? What do you mean share me? You told me last night it would be just you and me. You know that's what I want."

"But that was before your wolf found you. I know this is hard. I had it out with my dad over it, but as he reminded me, the well-being of the pack comes before that of the individual. And you know as well as I do that because full Lycan females are rare they are to be shared. At least your father and mine agreed to wait to add others until after we've conceived our first pup." A common practice as was genetic testing to track bloodlines and prevent inbreeding.

"How decent of you all to make that decision for me," she replied sarcastically.

"Dana, it's for the best."

"He beat you into agreeing to this, didn't he?" His bruises now made so much sense.

Nathan shrugged. "I'll admit I wasn't too keen on the idea at first. But Dad has a point, and your dad also made it a condition of his agreeing to our marriage. I'll take sharing you against your dad giving you to someone else any day."

Dana pushed out of his arms, aghast at his nonchalant attitude. She clung tightly to her anger to hide the breaking of her heart. "But you said it would be just you and me. You promised." She hated how pitiful she sounded. She hated even more that he didn't seem to care.

"It'll still be us, most of the time. And your dad says if I don't fight it, I'll get a vote when it comes to choosing the others. I'll make sure it's guys you'll like, like my best friend, John. You'll see. It won't be so bad."

Dana snapped, "Yes, it will be. It's not you who's got to whore himself out. I won't do it, and if you loved me, you wouldn't make me."

"I don't have a choice," he shouted back.

"Yes, you do. We could run away. Just you and me. Build a life together, away from the pack and its stupid laws." She gave him a chance. A chance to redeem himself. To prove his love to her.

"I can't do that. Where would we go? How would we live? And besides, you know I'm in line for the alpha position when my dad gets too old."

"So you're choosing the pack over me?" she asked in a quiet voice.

"No, I'm choosing both of you."

Dana shook her head. "No, you aren't. If you truly loved me, you wouldn't ask me to do this. Not knowing how much I hate the thought. Get out."

"Aw, come on, don't be like this, baby. You know I love you. I don't have a choice. It's pack law."

"Fuck you, and fuck the pack laws. Get out! Get out! Get out!" She punctuated her screams with the throwing of objects that she picked up randomly off her dresser.

Nathan stared at her in shock, letting the missiles bounce off him. "But I love you. Please, Dana, don't be like this."

"No, you don't love me," she wailed. "Get out. Please, just go." She collapsed to the floor, sobbing, unable to face his calm betrayal of what she'd thought was something pure. Something for them alone. Something special.

She heard a rustle, and she half expected to feel his hands on her, comforting her. Instead, she heard him say, "You'll get over it in time. You'll see once we're married and the babes start coming. It won't be so bad."

But she knew better. She'd watched it with her own mother. The smiles when it was just them and her dad. The stony face when the others came to claim their turn. The tears. The numerous miscarriages. And finally her death in childbirth.

Dana knew she was biased, given her mother's hysterics over being shared. She knew not all the women felt that way. Some even lived in perfect harmony with their numerous males, popping out babies. But all the happy ones in the world couldn't excuse those who had to be led in tears and drawn faces to do their duty for the pack.

Not me. I won't be shared. Her decision, while fine and dandy, though, didn't mean she'd get a say. She could beg, plead, and cry all she wanted. She already knew her father wouldn't listen. They'd give her no choice.

So she ran. With only the clothes on her back and the money she'd saved babysitting, she escaped the only life and family she'd known and exchanged it for a hard life.

* * * *

A lonely life. And one that twelve years later still made her question if it had been the right choice. As her mind went through its third cycle of the night that everything changed, she felt herself pulled from the dream. As she floated back to consciousness, she realized someone shook her gently while a persistent voice insisted she wake up. She slapped at the hand that tapped her cheek, her mind sluggish, and her eyelids held closed by a ton of bricks.

"Stop," she protested in a weak voice, forcing the words past a tongue that was thick and dry. She fuzzily wondered how she hadn't died. She remembered pain, lots of it. She also recalled her deep despair and the wish to end it all. She definitely didn't recall lying on a soft mattress like the one she found herself on now or the enticing smell of wolf that, for once, didn't make her want to bolt. Fear kept her eyes closed. What if she had died and was now in some sort of werewolf heaven?

"And here I thought you'd be eager to wake up and yell at me a little bit."

The familiar voice did what gentle cajoling couldn't. *Nathan?* A vague recollection of him in her cell, morphing from beast to man, floated to the surface of her mind. Could it be? Her eyes popped open. She didn't see Nathan, but the face bending over her seemed vaguely familiar. Handsome, with brown eyes that twinkled, the stranger smiled at her, and though she scented his Lycan nature, his calm demeanor didn't raise her hackles. Actually, her inner wolf stirred with interest. How unusual.

"Morning, Sleeping Beauty. Nice to see you're back with us." He offered her a bottle of water, and she grabbed it from him eagerly, slopping it wetly on herself as she drank, but she didn't care.

The cool liquid moistened her mouth and refreshed her, enough that she could ask, "Who are you? Where am I?" She withheld the third question. *Was that truly Nathan I heard? And if it was, am I happy or not that he's found me?*

"You probably don't remember me, but we ran into each other a few times in our younger pack years. My name's John."

The fuzzy wheels in her mind turned, and the answer popped up. "I know you. You're

Nathan's best friend. You used to be a lot skinnier." He'd remained cute, though. If Nathan hadn't asked her out after years of her mooning after him, she might have gone for his bookish friend. She still might. She found him quite attractive, and something about him made her relax, a feeling she hadn't enjoyed in what seemed like forever.

John grinned at her, displaying a dimple she found much too hot. "And geekier. You can say it. It was true then and still is now. As for being skinny, when I finally stopped growing, my body caught up. I'm surprised you even remember me, given you and Nathan were always off hiding in corners, necking."

Dana blushed at the reminder of her youth. "Yeah, well, that won't be happening again." She ignored the snort in the background and the way her heart stuttered. She spotted the stethoscope around John's neck. "Are you a doctor?"

"Yup. Mind if I check you over and make sure you're healing all right?"

His soft drawl made her tummy flip pleasantly. Even stranger, she didn't feel an urge to argue or refuse. *I must still be hurt.* "Okay."

His lips curved again, and she couldn't help but smile back, a smile that widened when she heard the impatient sigh from behind John.

She didn't fidget while John shone a light in her eyes and checked her pulse—a pulse that raced for numerous reasons. The doctor appeared to be having the oddest effect on her and distracted her almost as much as the man she sensed at the periphery of her vision. A man she refused to crane to see because that would smack too much of eagerness, and she was most definitely not eager to see him.

"I need to check your ribs. If you don't mind, I'm going to press them lightly. Let me know if they hurt."

She expected him to slip his hands under the sheet and cop a feel—she actually kind of looked forward to it so she could get indignant and erase these fuzzy feelings he engendered. But John acted a true gentleman and palpated her through the sheet, keeping his eyes trained to hers. Even through the thin fabric, though, her body temperature rose. *Oh, Doctor, I think I have a fever.* Dana wanted to giggle. The whole situation seemed surreal. Attracted to one werewolf while her body anxiously waited to see another. Had the beating she'd taken knocked her hatred of getting hooked up with a Lycan right out of her?

"You're healing well," her brown-eyed doctor declared, taking his hands away—and was it her, or did he do so reluctantly?

"How long was I out?" she asked as she inhaled and found only a slight hitch, whereas before breathing had resulted in burning agony.

"We ended up keeping you under for

about three days. You were injured pretty badly. Luckily, you only had fractures, so I didn't need to break and reset anything. We also managed to stem the internal bleeding until your healing abilities kicked in with the aid of some proteins fed via IV."

Three days! Dana didn't like knowing she'd lain so helpless for so long. And just where had they taken her? Anxiety hit her in a rush. "Awesome. Thanks for patching me up. Now if someone will just give me some clothes, I'll get out of your way." She threw that out there, knowing it would get a reaction. That and she really wanted some clothes, as she noticed she was pretty freaking naked under the damned sheets. *If anyone copped a feel, or more, while I was out, there is going to be hell to pay.* She blocked the mental images of gentle John touching her skin, seeing her naked form as he treated her.

Did he like what he saw? Not that she cared.

"Nice try, Dana." The deep voice set her limbs trembling, and she couldn't have said if it was fear or anticipation.

The doctor moved to the side, and Nathan came into view. Despite her apprehension, she drank him in, stunned with the shock of seeing him again.

He'd changed and yet hadn't. The same bright blue eyes stared at her, and he sported the same thick, dark mane of hair. But the boy she'd known was gone, replaced by a man, and a big one at that.

Apparently, he'd done some more growing after she left. He towered inches taller than she recalled and filled out his lanky frame, but not with fat. He bulged with muscle. He also looked hard, from the set of his jaw to the glint in his eye to the evident strength in his body. She suddenly feared this new man, this stranger she no longer knew but who had evidently sought her out. *For what purpose?*

"What do you want with me?" she asked in a voice that sounded weak and soft. She also wanted to slap herself for asking such a stupid question. She knew what he wanted, to bed her and impregnate her. But surely he could have found another woman in the years she'd been gone? Lycan females were rare, but given his evident alpha stature and good looks, the available ones would have fallen over themselves to snare him. Surprisingly, she didn't like this train of thought.

"Well, my dear fiancée, you ran off before we could be wed in the eyes of our people. I intend to rectify that delay as soon as possible, willing or not." He said it so matter-of-factly, so coldly, that it took her a moment to process it.

Her mouth dropped open. "Are you out of your fucking mind?"

"Yup."

His answer took her aback. Had Nathan

truly gone mad? She looked to John. "Tell me he's joking."

"John doesn't get a say," Nathan growled. "So stop looking at him. I'm the one you promised to mate with. I'm the one who saved your ass. I'm the one you will look to, not him."

She looked away from John, who shrugged apologetically. She faced Nathan again and saw the tic in the side of his jaw. *Is he jealous of John for some reason?* "No."

"No, what? Did you think you had a choice after the way you ran away from me?"

She narrowed her gaze and found her temper at last. "You betrayed me."

"I was a boy following the laws of my alpha. The laws we all follow."

"You could have said no." What she left unsaid was he could have chosen to run with her. He already knew that.

"Ah yes, you and your precious policy of not sharing regardless of our kind's laws and customs."

"Don't worry. You made that point abundantly clear. You'll be glad to know you win. Happy? I won't be sharing you with anyone else."

She heard the doctor utter an exclamation of surprise. "Nathan, the pack won't like that."

Nathan rounded on him. "I don't give a

fuck what the pack likes. I lost her once because I let the pack tell me what to do. I won't do it again. I'm alpha, and they'll do as I damned well say. And don't think I don't smell your interest in her. She's mine. I am invoking pack law on this one. She's unmated without a guardian to speak for her. Let it be known I claim her as mine."

Dana's temper simmered at his cave-wolf decree, and in exact reverse, her heart stuttered at his admission of regret. But change of mind or not, she wasn't about to reward him. He'd hurt her too badly, and now, she'd do the same right back. "Pack law is pack law. Isn't that what you once told me? Well, guess what. I'm also going to invoke your precious fucking pack law. I demand the right to a true pack mating." Dana invoked a clause rarely used, but one all girls were taught about by their mothers at a young age. In the case a Lycan female found herself of age to marry without a guardian, while a male could claim her, the female could request up to three more mates of her choice, a buffer of sorts in case the male who claimed her wasn't her first choice.

"What?" Both men whirled to face her, the doctor in surprise, Nathan in fury.

"You heard me, Nathan. Since you're going to force me to accept you as a mate, whether I want to or not, then I demand the right to choose three more mates. After all, it's for the good of the pack."

She embellished her saucy retort with a twisted smile. "And I'm starting with the good doctor over there, who, if my nose doesn't deceive me, is unmated."

"You can't do this," Nathan growled. "Do you have any idea how long I've looked for you? Waited to tell you I was sorry?"

"Gee, I guess you forgot the 'sorry' part when you ordered me around like some kind of slave to your wishes. Once again, it's all about you and what you want. What about what I want?" she yelled, clutching the sheet to her bosom before it fell and she gave them an eyeful.

"What's going on?" Another werewolf poked his head in, a rather good-looking one, and Dana pointed her finger at him.

"Him. I want him too."

"Dana!" Nathan bellowed, but she shot him the middle finger and a glare.

When another body jostled for position in the doorway, a tousled blond with a grin from ear to ear, she pointed again. "And that one for my fourth." She shot Nathan a triumphant grin.

"I won't share you," Nathan said through clenched teeth.

"Oh, sorry, was I ignoring what you want? Gee, what do you know? Payback's a bitch. Now if you men wouldn't mind, I need my rest if I'm expected to fuck you bunch of animals after you all claim me like some fucking prize."

She turned on her side and buried her face in the pillow, the tears hot as they spilled onto the fabric.

She could hear one of the men whispering, "What the hell just happened? Did I just get engaged?"

But the sound of their voices was quickly muffled as they closed the door—and locked it.

Alone, she gave in to tears. In truth, she understood Nathan had never had a chance against his father so many years ago.

But now that I've slapped him in the face with his betrayal, how the hell do I get out of it? She didn't actually want all the men—okay, that wasn't quite true. John actually really appealed to her, and seeing Nathan again only reinforced the fact that she'd never gotten over him. But still, revenge was one thing, mating with a bunch of strangers another. *I guess I'd better start planning my escape.* Somehow that idea held even less appeal. Had she changed so much in her years away that being bound to a bunch of guys was more appealing than a life of freedom—always on the run and never having roots?

Fuck me, what am I going to do?

Chapter Six

John followed Nathan's stiff body and knew they were in for trouble. They'd all expected her to balk at Nathan's plan, but nobody could have predicted she'd do an about-face and use pack law to choose more mates. Rarely used, it was an obscure clause that Lycan females of age with no guardian could invoke to surround herself with protection. The chosen males could actually say no, but, and this was where the fight would begin, John had no interest in saying no. John wanted Dana with an intensity he'd never expected or experienced. And while Jeffrey, one of her impromptu choices, might back out, given he was quite smitten with a human girl in town, John could already tell Kody didn't mind the idea at all of being mated with the feisty Dana.

Nathan was going to freak.

They followed Nathan's stiff back down the stairs to the main floor. Nathan whirled once they hit the cavernous living room with its floor-to-ceiling windows.

"Unfucking real. She's doing this just to punish me. You will, of course, all refuse her."

Eve Langlais

Nathan glared at them all around, and while Jeffrey raised his hands in surrender, John met his stare head-on, as did Kody. "Are you defying me?" Nathan growled.

"Hey, don't look at me. I refuse, and I'm outta here," said Jeffrey with a wave as he booked it for the door.

Kody crossed his arms and leaned against the wooden support for the balcony that ringed the living room on the second floor. "I don't see what the big deal is. All the other females in the pack have multiple mates. What makes Dana different?"

"She's mine."

"I don't think we're contesting your right to be first," John interjected, although if Dana expressed a desire otherwise—say she wanted him first—John would fight to respect her wishes. His wolf would not let him do any less. It would seem friendship stretched only so far when the woman he and his wolf wanted as mate became an issue. But John hoped it wouldn't come to that. Nathan would eventually come to his senses, and by that, he meant obeying pack law whether Nathan's jealousy could handle it or not.

"I'm going to be her one and only. It's what she wants," Nathan said, crossing his arms over his chest with an obstinate look.

"Not according to what she said," Kody sassed back. John realized that the younger man

70

must have been listening and made sure he got in on the fiasco.

"She was mad." Nathan looked pained, and while John felt for him, he still wouldn't back down.

John shrugged. "Mad or not, until she takes it back, I, for one, am not going to refuse. She's not only strong and beautiful, according to my wolf, she's the one. I'd be stupid to turn her down because you can't handle your jealousy."

Nathan's brows arched high in surprise. "I handled my fucking jealousy so well last time that she ran the hell away. It took me twelve goddamn years to find her. I am not, I repeat not, going to do anything that's going to make her run again."

"Yeah, 'cause your whole 'me Tarzan, you Jane' routine where you thumped your chest upstairs like some caveman really impressed her," Kody piped in sarcastically. "Did it ever occur to you that you scare her? It's been a long time, man, and you gotta admit you're a lot bigger than you used to be. Maybe she wants us as some kind of shield."

"I would never hurt her." Nathan's voice came out almost in a whisper, and his shoulders slumped.

"In her mind, you already have," John said, quietly hitting him with the truth.

With a bellow of rage, Nathan snapped and charged at John. Not as big, John nevertheless met his charge head-on. Where rage drove Nathan, John relied on cool logic.

They exchanged slugs, Nathan venting his frustration and John prodding him to make sure he got a good workout. He took his bruises like a man and gave several of his own as he let his best friend work out his jealousy and grief over finding out the woman he'd moped about for years hadn't harbored the same feelings.

They might have gone at it for a while had Kody not announced, "Thought you guys might want to know she's trying to escape."

The startling announcement made John's attention waver, and Nathan clocked him with a hard right hook. John staggered, and Nathan pushed past him for the stairs. John, without thinking, stuck his foot out and tripped him. Nathan fell with a crash, and John scrambled to get over him, only to have Nathan yank him down.

They tussled on the floor for a second before John, in a moment of clarity, said, "Um, Kody's gone after her—by himself."

Nathan went still. "He's going to steal a kiss, isn't he?"

John nodded, and that quickly they went from fighting to in cahoots. They tore up the stairs, two at a time, to the room they'd locked her in. And found it still locked. Nathan fumbled the key out, but John didn't wait. He tore down the hall to his bedroom and right through to his window. He threw up the sash and peered out just in time to see her hit the ground in a tuck and roll that brought her right to Kody's feet.

She's certainly determined to keep us on our toes, he thought with a grin that turned into outright laughter as Kody leaned in for a peck, only to get his smooch returned with a crushing left hook.

Hot damn, I wonder if she'll be as energetic in bed. He couldn't wait to find out.

* * * *

Dana didn't allow herself to cry with self-pity for long. Tears wouldn't fix anything; only action might. Dana realized she probably couldn't get away, but that wouldn't stop her from trying. The guys might have left and locked her in, but doors weren't the only way out. She dove out of the bed, toward the chest of drawers she saw. She rummaged through the male clothing—smelling disturbingly of Nathan—and yanked out a T-shirt that hung down to her knees. Not that she cared.

She found some black briefs, but they threatened to slide right down her legs. She yanked them off and pitched them across the room. Screw it. A proper escape didn't require underwear. She headed to the window when she spotted a familiar duffel bag. *They grabbed my stuff?*

She unzipped and, sure enough, found her clothing. Quickly, she stripped the large T-shirt and dressed in her own stuff. She kept her ears peeled for Nathan's return, but while she heard a lot of yelling and thumping, she didn't sense anyone coming.

She zipped the duffel bag back up and went to the window. She threw up the sash and peered out. High, but she'd jumped from higher when the situation called for it. And being engaged to four men certainly fit the bill.

She debated taking her duffel with her, but it would just slow her down. She straddled the window ledge, cursing as a wave of dizziness chose that moment to hit.

"Come on, don't be a wuss now," she coaxed herself. She regulated her breathing and, closing her eyes against the weakness flooding her, thrust her second leg out. She maneuvered herself so that she slid her body off the edge while using her fingertips to grip the ledge. She counted to three and took a deep breath before letting go, only belatedly praying that her body had healed enough to handle the impact. She didn't plummet long before she hit the ground with a slight wince. Years of practice had taught her to flex and tumble into a roll that had her springing up and ramming into a rock-hard wall.

Startled, she flailed backward but didn't fall. Strong hands gripped her, and she opened her eyes to see the tousled blond from earlier grinning at her.

"Darling, if you wanted me, you could have just called me."

Dana could only gape at him stupidly.

Then the blond Lycan kissed her. Butterflies fluttered in her tummy, and Dana blamed it on her exertion. But as he deepened his kiss and her cleft moistened, panic set in. *Attracted to John, Nathan, and now this young pup?*

Shock at her body's betrayal brought her to her senses, and she pulled back from the mouth that caressed her so expertly while, at the same time, bringing up her hand to strike a solid blow.

His head snapped back, but instead of loosening his grip on her, his hands tightened. She waited for the return slap. The yelling. The shaking. Instead, the blond wolf laughed.

"Hot damn, darling. That's some left hook you got there."

"You shouldn't have kissed me." She spoke the words, but her tingling lips wanted to pout when he didn't resume his caress.

His green eyes twinkled at her. "I was just sealing the engagement, darling. And might I say, I think you've made a fine choice."

"But-but—" She wanted to protest it was a mistake, but before she could utter a coherent sentence, she found herself yanked from his grasp.

"Caught you," Nathan growled before he upended and threw her over his shoulder, its width digging into her belly.

"Put me down," she screeched.

"Not fucking likely," snarled Nathan, following it with a slap on her bottom.

Though stunned at his action, she didn't cry out because it hadn't hurt, but then the indignity of her situation set in. She lost it.

"You fucking prick! Set me down right this instant." She called him several choice names, punctuated with jabs to his lower back, some hard enough to make him grunt, but he didn't reply and just smacked her hard on the bottom again.

She gave an inarticulate cry of rage. She looked wildly to her left, saw nobody to help, and looked to the other side to see John striding alongside.

"Make him put me down," she appealed to him.

John frowned at her. "You are still healing, woman. Do you realize what kind of damage you might have done with that stunt?"

Actually, she did know because her ribs ached something awful. Defeated—for the moment—she stopped fighting and hung there limply. When she was laid with more gentleness than expected back in the bed, she turned her face to the side and refused to look at anyone.

"I need to examine her," she heard John

say softly.

"And?" Nathan bit out.

"Nathan, get out. She's hurt again, so you needn't worry anything is going to happen. Besides, shouldn't you be posting a guard outside the window so she doesn't get the drop on us again?"

"Touch her and die," Nathan growled.

"You don't get a say," she snapped, turning to face him.

"Don't test me, Dana, or I'll mark you as mine right this instant."

"Do that, and the first time you try to come to my bed, I'll rip your fucking dick off."

Nathan clenched his fists and jaw, but Dana glared right back. She wouldn't be forced or threatened.

"We'll discuss this again later," he finally managed to say through gritted teeth.

Dana watched his stiff back as he tread heavily across the room and slammed the door shut. She let out a breath she hadn't realized she'd been holding, for despite her vehement opposition to his domineering threat to claim her, a part of her was aroused by it.

"All right, little missy. Time to see what damage you've done. Lift your shirt."

Dana whipped her head around and glared at him. "Like fuck. Do your stuff with my shirt on, like you did earlier."

John's brown eyes held her gaze, and he

gave her a stern look. "Before, I wasn't worried about internal bleeding. But now, because you decided to act like an idiot, I need to check for bruising that might indicate internal problems, not to mention make sure you didn't re-snap your ribs."

Dana hated his logical answer. But even she wasn't stupid enough to defy a doctor, not when he could be right. She turned her gaze to stare at the ceiling and pulled her shirt up. His hands palpated her, and this time, without the barrier of the fabric, the heat of his touch immediately ignited her.

"Why did you do it?" he asked softly.

"Isn't it obvious? I'm not interested in being mated with a bunch of guys."

"And what if we were to forget your earlier request to claim us and it was just Nathan?"

"I don't want him either. I don't want anybody. I want to live my own life."

"Ah yes, because the situation you were in when we found you was so much better."

"At least I was free," she retorted, tilting to look at him. She found him watching her, and something warm pooled in her lower stomach.

"Care to rephrase that? As I recall, when we found you, there were chains."

Dana blushed. "Before those thugs caught me, I was living a perfectly fine life. I made my own decisions, did what I wanted. I was free."

John snorted. "You call that freedom? I saw your house with its alarms and lack of personal touches. It looked like a prison to me, one built on paranoia and fear."

His remark stabbed her with its truth. In running for her freedom, had she inadvertently caged herself tighter? "So what do you suggest? That I give up my identity? Give up my rights to become a whore for a bunch of horny wolves?"

John shook his head, and his lips curved. "Did it ever occur to you that if you were mated, you'd enjoy more freedom? With the mark of one, you'd avoid the problems of males trying to claim you. Become marked by more and you'd have your own built-in defense system to ensure you could do anything you wanted."

"Oh please, like I'd be allowed to do anything other than suck cock and pop out babies," she replied crudely.

"You have a really warped idea of what being mated with multiple males is like." John shook his head at her.

"So tell me how you see it then."

His gaze softened along with his voice. "I'll tell you how I saw it growing up. My mother wanted for nothing. Anything she needed, my fathers got for her. Every evening, after they put the children to bed, they'd sit, either on the porch or in the living room, and talk."

"And they took turns fucking?" Dana used the crude phrase to remind herself that the beautiful picture he'd painted was nothing like the life she'd seen growing up.

"They made love, you mean. Sometimes my mother would take only one of my fathers to bed. Sometimes she'd take them all. But I can tell you one thing. Every morning she came down those stairs with a smile on her face. She still does."

"So it works for some people. It wouldn't work for me. I want an emotional connection with someone before I bed them."

"Fine. I can wait for that."

She met his gaze and could read only sincerity in their depths. *Don't tell me I actually believe him? He's a man. He'd say anything to get in my pants.* "You're assuming I'll go through with the whole marking thing."

"I think you will. I think, regardless of your fighting words, that you're tired of running. Why not stay? Give it a try. You might be surprised."

Dana shifted restlessly. She could handle yelling and arguing. His calm discussion took her unaware, and she didn't know how to fight back. "What, and become some mindless robot wolf who thinks that polygamy is all right just because it's the way things are done?"

John appeared to ponder his next words. "I'll admit, even having grown up with it, and seeing it in such a positive light, I wasn't too sure if that's what I wanted for myself. There is something to be said about not sharing. But at the same time, the sense of family, the built-in companionship, it is quite tempting. Even more so when you find the right woman and realize that, unless you're willing to share her, you won't get a chance."

Is he saying I'm that woman? The concept should have made her curl her lip and spit in his direction. Instead, her cheeks bloomed with color before reality slapped her. "Nathan will never go for it. He just wants me in his bed and doesn't care how I feel about it." *And even odder, I'm no longer sure how I feel about it.* Before the kidnapping, she'd have said never would she take him back, not in a million years. However, now that she faced with him again, feelings long buried rose to the surface, and they were saying maybe it was time for something new. Something that didn't leave her blinking back tears of loneliness. Time for a life where running was done for pleasure and not to save her life.

"Leave Nathan to me." John's hands had stopped stroking her skin at the start of their conversation, but they now resumed checking her ribs. Dana gasped when he pressed a sore spot.

"Sorry," he murmured. He leaned down and placed a light kiss on the area that hurt. Lust shot through her like a bolt of lightning, and she gasped again for an entirely different reason.

John didn't stop his sensual caress, but neither did he grow bolder. Lightly, he trailed his mouth over her ribs, stopping at the hem of her T-shirt. He pulled it down with his teeth, covering her. She almost wailed, *Why are you stopping?*

She closed her eyes as her cheeks heated. He brushed his lips against hers. The barest touch, but it made her shiver down to her toes. "I look forward to becoming friends and, in time, when you're ready, lovers."

Then he left. The soft thud of the door shutting had her opening her eyes to find herself alone with only the tingling touch of his lips to remind her she hadn't dreamed it.

Could it be like he says? Could I be happy? What he'd described sounded so beautiful, happy, and, best of all, peaceful. But was it even a possibility?

She wanted to deny her attraction to the men she'd engaged herself to. Well, three of them anyway. The redhead didn't actually draw her like the others. He'd just been convenient during her vengeful tantrum. But the blond with the dancing green eyes who'd kissed her? John who calmed her inner turmoil? And Nathan whom she'd never stopped wanting and, even in her current anger, made her long for him?

Is this what I want? To chain myself to these men, to bed all of them? John had struck a nerve when he'd called her previous life a prison. Content didn't equate with happy. With her blood rushing through her, her body aroused, her mind whirling, she felt more alive than she had in all the years she'd embraced her freedom.

But she didn't want to rush into things, to make a decision based on hormones and possibly vulnerability from her attack. She needed time to decide. Time to reevaluate her mindset on the whole polygamy scenario. Time to see if these men could make her happy.

Chapter Seven

Nathan hit the punching bag over and over again. It wasn't working to clear up his frustration, but he felt better for smacking something.

I handled it all so fucking wrong.

He'd cared for Dana so tenderly during her convalescence, acted the perfect gentlemen as he'd lifted her for bathing and other private necessities that would have surely made her blush had she known. He'd wanted to care for her himself, but had grudgingly allowed John, who had the medical expertise, to monitor and treat her. He'd restrained himself from punching the lights out of his best friend when he noted how his friend lingered over her, his eyes alight with an expression Nathan recognized all too well.

But he'd consoled himself with the fact that, once Dana woke, he'd talk to her, apologize for not standing firmer against their fathers, make her understand he'd do anything to make her forgive him because he couldn't live without her.

Nathan had tried to forget Dana, but

scores of women in his bed couldn't erase her memory. They'd sated a basic need. However, none came close to filling the hole in his heart and soul.

He'd determined if the only way to get Dana back was to keep her to himself, then so be it. He'd kill any who opposed his plan to selfishly keep all her love for him alone. *I'm the alpha of this pack. If they don't like it, then they can line up for a beating.* As for the Lycan council, they owed him with all the favors he'd done for them. Surely they wouldn't begrudge him claiming and keeping to himself the woman he loved.

He'd had it all planned, from his apology to her tearful acceptance, followed by his joyous marking and claiming of her. A great plan until she'd woken and he'd seen the looks she'd exchanged with John, sensed her interest in another male—an interest reciprocated. Jealousy had consumed him and then spoken for him. With words, he'd laid claim to her in a Neanderthal fashion that had backfired so badly.

She didn't want him. Or if she did, she hid it well. She'd chosen others, and while a part of him acknowledged she did it out of revenge and hurt, it didn't change the fact. She'd set the rules. He'd have to share her.

He no longer knew if he was capable of that.

A tap on his shoulder made him whirl, and he saw John.

"Let's spar while we talk." John inclined his head toward the open area in the gym, and Nathan followed too eagerly, his fists all too willing to *talk* to his supposed best friend.

They both dropped into a fighter's stance and circled each other, seeking an opening.

John began the verbal one. "We need to talk about Dana."

"What's there to say? She hates me and wants you." Bitterness colored his words.

"She's hurt and confused," John replied with a jab that went wide.

"Gee, I hadn't noticed."

"She still cares for you beneath her anger."

Nathan swung hard and hit the arm John brought up to block. "Great. I feel so much better. And how's that going to help me when you end up fucking her because she likes you more right now?"

John stopped moving and glared at him. "It's that attitude that's going to fuck it up for all of us."

"That's it. Blame me for everything. If I'm such an asshole, then why not just claim her for yourself?"

"Goddamn it, Nathan. Would you stop acting like a fucking child? Yes, I think she might want me, but guess what. I know she wants you too. She might have asked for a true mating in the heat of anger, but I think there's a chance she might actually go through with it."

Nathan dropped his guard, and John jabbed him in the midsection. Nathan wheezed and danced back, trying to catch enough breath to speak. "What makes you think that?"

"She's tired of running. She just wants to be happy, but because of something in her past, she seems to think that's not possible in a true mated relationship."

Nathan blocked some shots and threw a few of his own, wondering how much he should reveal of Dana's upbringing. With a sigh at his stupidity in refusing the truce his friend offered, he told him the unvarnished truth. "Dana's dad was a dick. Probably why he got along so well with my old man. He treated his wife like shit, and the men he shared her with were no better. Not just that, but he shared her with any buddy who showed up to visit."

"Are you fucking kidding me? That's sick. The mating bond is supposed to be sacred between those who've marked her."

"Yeah, well, we all know that's not always the case. My dad knew he was doing it and did nothing to stop it. Said it was none of his business how Ted and the others treated their wife. Needless to say, Dana's mom wasn't a happy person."

"It explains why Dana has such a poor

view of the whole thing."

"Yeah. She thinks that all ménages are like that. I never bothered explaining otherwise at the time. I never thought it would be an issue, given she was a dormant until I took her maidenhead."

"No wonder she freaked. Watching her own mother live in misery because of it . . ." John shook his head. "I heard her mother miscarried quite a bit until she finally died of it."

Nathan shifted uncomfortably, and John used this to his advantage to slide under his guard and bruise his ribs.

"What are you hiding?" John demanded, stopping to face him with stormy eyes.

"She did miscarry, but it wasn't the babe that killed her but Dana's father. Dana was the only babe that made it. Her mother lost almost a dozen babes after her. Ted blamed her. Claimed she was doing something to kill them in her womb."

John snorted with disgust. "Sounds more like they didn't give her body time to heal before trying again."

"Could be. Anyway, her dad beat Dana's mother after the last one, bad enough she never recovered and died."

The horror in John's eyes mirrored the ache in his heart. "Does she know?"

"I don't think so, but she might have suspected. Her dad wasn't one to hide the fact he was a dick."

John rubbed his face. "Well, this would certainly explain her attitude. We're going to have our work cut out trying to convince her it can work."

"It'd be easier if you and Kody butted out." Nathan threw it out there, even as he knew the answer. Once a man's wolf caught scent of his mate, nobody else would do.

John grinned at him. "You wish. What's wrong? Afraid of a little competition?"

Nathan wanted to be pissed that his friend found the situation so funny, but instead of hitting him, a chuckle burst free. "Ha, you don't stand a chance. I know her weak spot."

John held his hand out, and Nathan clasped it then yanked the man who was like a brother to him for a hug. It lasted only a moment. They were, after all, men.

John laughed. "Good thing we like each other because if we can convince her to stay, we're going to be together a long time. Think we'll ever get her to open up enough for her to take more than one of us at once?"

Nathan, who'd have said never in a million years a few days ago, now had to wonder. Dana had changed, and he could no longer say with certainty what she would or wouldn't do.

As for him, the idea of a ménage intrigued him. While he was a true lover of the female form, there was something to be said about the eroticism of a group orgy that made him hope that one day Dana would be open enough to try.

"If we do ever get that lucky, that puppy Kody better not be there. If what I hear is true, he'd put us both to shame."

John looked down at his crotch ruefully. "Damn. That would explain the number of ladies always hanging about looking for him."

Nathan laughed. Maybe things wouldn't turn out so badly, so long as he was first to mark her and claim her with his cock. That wasn't something he was willing to relinquish.

Chapter Eight

Dana paced the bedroom, torn between annoyance and anticipation. After her failed escape attempt and titillating exam by John, she'd napped. A nap that left her hot and bothered and, even worse, more confused than ever. Her dreams were filled with men, familiar ones bent on seducing her, touching her, pleasing her—all at once. And damned if she didn't find it hot. But at the same time, she didn't know what to do about it.

Dana was fast approaching thirty-one, and yet she embarrassingly lacked sexual experience. Her maiden voyage, so to speak, with Nathan was her one and only attempt at lovemaking. Not because she didn't desire sex or intimacy,. She just hadn't found anyone else who drew her in the twelve years she'd hidden. Inexperience, however, didn't mean she was completely clueless. She'd taken to reading romance novels and erotica. She became quite adept at masturbation, touching herself in a quick frenzy that didn't completely satisfy her. However, a self-induced orgasm was one thing, a mind-shattering experience like the one she remembered at Nathan's hands a whole other. Despite her misgivings, despite her confusion and, yes, even fear, she longed to taste that passion again. The most shocking part, she didn't just desire Nathan. She'd jumped to the extreme and found herself wanting three men— possibly at once.

Dana had never understood the whole ménage thing in the bedroom. In her world, it was one man, one woman at a time. She'd avoided books of that type due to her pack experience. But ever since John had spoken to her, she couldn't stop thinking about it, wondering how it would feel. To end up the focus of so many hands, tongues, and cocks . . .

Her train of thought appalled her, yet it also excited her. Could she find pleasure in such a naughty scenario? How would the mechanics of it work? Who would put what where? How could she even contemplate it?

Could I try it without binding myself as their mate? A trial run, so to speak? She bit her lip at the naughty thought.

She wore a path in the rug with her back-and-forth pacing. So intent was she with her inner dialogue that she didn't hear someone enter.

"Thinking of me, darling?" said a voice from right behind her.

Dana screamed and whirled. With a survival instinct cultivated over twelve years on the run, she thrust and kicked without pause. And both her shots connected. The blond pup who had snuck up on her folded over and hit the floor groaning.

Dana immediately felt contrite and dropped to the floor beside him. "I'm sorry. You scared the hell out of me."

A heart-stopping moment later, she found herself yanked on top of him. She peered at him in shock and saw him watching her back with a wide grin. He was also very happy to see her, judging by the thickness that nudged the apex of her thighs. If the tingling that raced through her body at his proximity was any indication, her body didn't mind and, in fact, rejoiced.

"I'll forgive you for a kiss," he said.

Dana almost laughed. His outrageous claim should have put her hackles up, but he truly did look adorable lying there with his blond hair in disarray and twinkling green eyes. His lips quirked at her perusal, and she found herself unconsciously moving closer, caving in to his request. As soon as she realized it, twelve years of habit kicked in. She halted herself and smiled sweetly. "Not likely." Then, offering a mental apology, she kneed him.

She didn't stop to admire his lovely shade of purple, although she did cringe as she heard him gasp for air as she fled out the open bedroom door and ran smack-dab into an implacable chest.

"Caught you. Again."

Dana sighed as she looked up at Nathan, who steadied her with hands that kept the sizzle in her body going. *Damned hormones.* She expected to see storm clouds in his eyes at her impromptu flight, but instead, he met her gaze with a smile so sweet it made her knees wobble. He mistook her sudden swaying for something else and tightened his grasp on her.

"Are you all right?"

She couldn't answer with words but did blush as her action of the previous moment caught up to her.

"Where's Kody?" he asked, his smile fading. "Did he do something?"

"Who?" Then she clicked in. "Oh, if you mean Blondie, he's having a private moment with his nuts right now." Nathan winced, and she grinned. "Care to join him?"

He dropped his hands from her and stepped back. Dana could almost see him mentally debating whether to cup his hands over his groin or not. "I thought I'd give him a hand escorting you down to dinner. I'm beginning to think I should have brought John too."

"Wimp." She pushed past him, shivering at the electricity that coursed through her body at the simple touch.

"Hot damn, Nathan. I think she broke

me."

Dana bit her lip as she heard Kody moaning he'd never make love again. *Well, that would be a shame, because, by the feel of him, he's got a lot of love to give.*

She made it down the stairs and then stopped dead at the view. Floor-to-ceiling windows spanned the two stories of the home and looked out over a forest. The house, perched on some kind of bluff, had a fantastic view, which somehow seemed familiar. *But I don't remember ever being in a house like this.*

"Beautiful, isn't it?" Nathan's breath tickled her ear. He'd snuck up on her, and she barely held in a startled shriek. "I had it built specifically for you. I remember how you used to love coming to this spot and holding out your arms and claiming that, when you stood there, you felt like the queen of the forest."

Dana turned to look at him. "You remember that? God, I was only, like, eight when I used to play that game. I didn't even think you knew I existed back then."

"Oh, I knew. I might not have shown it until you were older, but I always kept an eye on you."

His confession disturbed her, and Dana turned away again to move closer to the windows. Now that he'd pointed it out, she could recognize some landmarks while other areas looked alien. The forest had grown considerably in her absence, and the realization of their location made tears prick her eyes. "You brought me back to the compound."

"I brought you home," he corrected.

Dana couldn't face him with her eyes wet. Instead, she reached a hand out and touched the cold glass. "Home for you, maybe. But to me it was a hell I couldn't wait to escape." Especially once Nathan betrayed her.

"I can't change the past, Dana. I wish I could if it would make things right between us."

"Yeah, well, you know what my dad used to say about wishes. Speaking of whom, where is that old bastard? I'm surprised he's not here with a silver leash to make sure I do his bidding." Dana couldn't help the bitterness when she thought of her father. She'd had years to realize his treatment of her was unhealthy and abusive. Even now, as a grown woman, she shivered at the fear he'd trap her and force her to do his bidding, make her life a living hell.

"He's dead, Dana. He died of liver disease about three years after you left. He can't hurt you anymore."

Dana had speculated on what had happened to her father over the years she'd lived in hiding and woken up more than once in a cold sweat thinking he'd found her and brought his thick leather belt. She'd also asked herself many a time how she'd feel if he died. With Nathan's announcement, she queried her emotions—and felt . . . *nothing. Wait, that's not true. I'm glad that miserable bastard died.*

"Well, that's the first bit of good news I've heard," she announced a tad too brightly.

"Dana—" Nathan reached to grab her, but she spun away from him. She didn't need comforting.

"I'm fine, Nathan."

"I know you guys didn't always get along, but it's okay to mourn him."

Dana gaped at him. "Didn't get along? The man was a sick pig. Remember how your dad used to beat you? Well, guess what. So did mine."

Nathan frowned. "What are you talking about? I know he was strict, but I would have remembered seeing bruises."

Dana laughed, the shrill sound a little crazed. "My father knew better than to mark a female Lycan where others would see. Even a dormant one. He did it where people wouldn't see, using his fists or his belt depending on his mood. A shirt and pants cover backs and asses. It didn't make his abuse any less real."

The pity in Nathan's eyes made her want to cry. "I didn't know."

"And so what if you had? What would you have done?"

"Killed him," he said in a dark voice.

"Too late. The alcohol beat you to it. So, now maybe you understand why I think the

97

world is a better place with him gone. Thanks for making my day. Are we done hashing the past? I'm starved. Where's the food? I assume you Neanderthals ordered in."

"Did anyone ever tell you that you are a feminist? Just because we're men doesn't mean we can't handle ourselves in a kitchen." John's soothing voice from behind her somehow sucked some of her anger away. *The man is like walking Prozac.*

Dana turned to see John enter the living room brandishing a wooden spoon. She couldn't help but smile at him, thankful for his timely interruption. "Oh please, don't tell me you're a doctor and you cook?"

John brandished the spoon with mock menace then smiled sheepishly. "Actually, I just stir. Nathan there is the true chef while Kody is the pastry king."

Dana pivoted back to Nathan, who shrugged. "I needed a hobby to occupy me when you left. Apparently I can't bash heads in every day."

Dana shook her head. Nathan just kept surprising her and reminded her just how little she'd truly known about him. Actually, how little they'd known about each other.

Kody, who'd made it down the stairs, if somewhat ashen-faced, waved at her and even managed a smile.

Chagrin enveloped her, especially when

she realized he wasn't going to yell at her for hurting him so badly. "I'm sorry. Instincts, you know." She shrugged and gave him a small smile.

"Forget it, darling. As one of your chosen, I count myself lucky because I know you held back from causing permanent damage. Although, if you insist on kissing it better, I won't argue."

Dana's mouth rounded into an *O* of surprise, and before she knew it, she'd grabbed a carved figurine from a side table and whipped it at Kody, who caught it without batting an eye.

"I hope we get this mating thing over with quick because I'm beginning to doubt my ability to survive the courtship," Kody said, turning the statue over in his hands.

Dana knew the right thing at that moment was to tell Kody, and even John, for that matter, that she had no intention of taking any of them as a mate, including Nathan, but she didn't want to. Not just yet at least.

She didn't want to analyze her reasons too closely, but one thing became glaringly obvious. This was the most fun she'd had in years. Even stranger, even though she had three Lycans vying for her affection, she didn't feel threatened in any way. Actually, the knot of tension from always being on the lookout had loosened since she'd woken in their care.

Oh, fuck me, don't tell I'm going to cave to my

hormones and let all three of them mark me. Although, if she took all three as her mates at once, it would make for an interesting wedding night.

Looking around at the three guys, she frowned. "What happened to the fourth guy?"

"That other guy is called Jeff, and he's graciously declined your offer, given he's just about engaged to someone else," John replied, tucking her hand in his arm to lead her to the dining area.

Dana held in her sigh of relief at the news. She had enough troubles trying to figure a way out of the mess she found herself in—and imagine ways for it to get more twisted and naked—to worry about a fourth possible suitor. But she didn't let them know that. "Oh. Well, I'm sure I'll find someone else to complete our happy little family."

Nathan growled. Kody laughed, and John just patted her hand. "See, I knew you'd come around to the whole multi-mate thing. The more, the merrier. Just think of all the tongues in play."

And with those shocking words from the doctor she'd mistaken for calm, she was seated. *Now if only I was hungry for food instead of the picture he just painted in my mind.*

* * * *

Kody hung back as Nathan and John

flanked Dana, enjoying the swaying view of Dana's ass. *Hot damn, I can't wait to sink into that.*

Kody refused to view his throbbing cock from her earlier attempt to incapacitate him as a setback. A lesson, yes, but one well worth it given what he'd learned. One, Dana wasn't as immune to him as she pretended. Two, she felt bad about hurting him. Three, she had the cutest blush when embarrassed, and he couldn't wait to see it on her face when he fucked her for the first time. And four, not only did she ooze with beauty she also possessed a deadly side to her that didn't take any shit.

Other men might have shied from her violent side or, worse, tried to beat it out of her. Kody, however, liked that she had spirit and didn't fear standing up for herself. He'd seen too many women who thought nothing of letting men walk all over them. Not that she needed to worry about that with him. Kody had only the greatest of respect for women, in and out of bed, despite his naughty innuendos. He'd never imagined getting collared so young, but from the moment he'd laid eyes on Dana, an urge to claim her and protect her had almost overwhelmed him—and made his usually placid wolf pace in his mind. Folks talked about love at first sight—or the mating instinct at first scent—and Kody had laughed. No longer.

He and his inner wolf couldn't wait to put their mark on Dana and sink his cock into her glorious heat. Sure, given her prickly nature, they would probably butt heads on a regular basis, but he could almost guarantee the makeup sex after would rock both their worlds.

The fact that he'd have to share her with Nathan and John didn't bother him. Raised in a pack to the west that religiously followed pack law in regards to multi-partner matings, he had always expected if he found the one that he'd end up one of several. He counted himself lucky that he both liked and respected the men he'd share the mating bond with. While he was a few years younger than Nathan and John, they'd still become good friends, and if he was to become part of a polyamorous group, they were the men he most trusted to share that intimate joining.

Kody did have some reservations, though. He knew Dana had previously run because she didn't want to adhere to the pack law stating Lycan females had to take more than one male to mate. He also knew she'd initially chosen him out of revenge against Nathan. However, she'd had time since to change her mind. He hoped she didn't, but he'd respect her choice. He had enough cocky self-assurance, though, to think that, while she might hem and haw initially, she eventually just wouldn't be able to help herself.

Dana aside, though, there were other issues with the whole multi-mate scenario. John was on board, and Kody knew that he wouldn't run into issues in that quarter. But Nathan . . . Nathan was a whole other ball game. He'd tried to warn Kody away earlier in the day, claiming Dana had said she'd only chosen him out of anger. Kody had only to remember the kiss when he'd caught her outside to know, whatever her initial intention, she wanted him. So regardless of what Nathan wanted or said, Kody considered himself one of her mates-in-waiting until she said otherwise. He'd suffer the bruises Nathan would bestow for that privilege. Besides, he'd probably end up getting them kissed better.

Once Dana did make up her mind to exchange marks with them and everyone got on board, they'd get to the fun part—hot and sweaty sex. Kody wondered if she'd only indulge in the one-on-one type of fun or if she would be more adventurous and allow them to love her as a group. Kody himself had only ever participated in ménages with human girls, so his experience was somewhat limited. He was game to try, though, with men, so long as everyone kept their dicks and hands on Dana. Else he'd have to reassert his masculinity by punching a few faces.

Even if she chose to take them on solo, he didn't really care, so long as he got to sink into Dana and feel her nails raking down his back. Thoughts of her body under his as he plowed her brought on an instant erection that made him casually drop his hands and cross them over his groin.

The dinner table shuffle made him grin as both John and Nathan made sure they ended up seated on either side of her, which left Kody the spot he wanted, right across from her. He sat down and quietly helped himself to the grub. Nathan had gone all out trying to impress Dana. He'd made a succulent roast dripping with juice, roasted potatoes with rosemary, buttery carrots, and hot rolls. Kody groaned in exaggeration as he ate, drawing giggles from Dana, who ate her food with wide-eyed surprised. Nathan perhaps ruled strictly as pack alpha and acted like a man obsessed when around or talking about Dana, but when it came to food, hot damn, the man could cook.

The conversation flowed in jerks and halts.

"This is really good," she said. "I still can't believe you made this."

Kody spoke before Nathan could, which earned him a glare. "I'll admit the man is a genius when it comes to food, but my desserts will make you cream." Kody grinned at her, a grin that widened when her cheeks turned bright pink. For a tough-as-nails woman, when talk turned sexual, she blushed quite endearingly.

Nathan and John took over the conversation, and Kody let them. He'd achieved his desired result—getting her attention. Kody kept an eye on her as he ate, absently listening as his pack brothers caught her up on pack news since she'd left. Dana appeared nervous—from the way she kept licking her lips, the slight tremble in her hand, and, even yummier, the faint scent of her arousal.

Kody bided his time, watching as she got more and more flushed. Nathan and John kept touching her, innocent caresses for the most part, that made her all too aware of them—brushing her hand or arm as she reached for something, leaning sideways to whisper things in her ear that made her blush and cream, a tantalizing aroma Kody knew they could all smell.

She could deny it until she turned blue in the face. Dana was horny, his favorite state of being, which meant the time had arrived for him to up the ante.

Kody slipped off his shoes under the table, and lifting a leg, he used his foot to nudge her legs apart. Her startled eyes rose from her plate to meet his. Before she could open her mouth to say anything, he straightened his leg and placed his foot right against her mound and pressed against her. Her eyes went slightly out of focus. Encouraged, he rubbed his foot against the crotch of her jeans, her heat clearly evident even through the layers of material separating them.

He held his breath as he waited for her to throw a knife at him—he had one hand ready to catch it. He even readied to yank his foot back in case she decided to jab it, but as he continued to press and rub against her covered pussy, she did nothing.

Well, not completely. Her eyes dilated. Her cheeks flushed. Her breathing quickened, and the scent of her arousal increased. Kody could see the puzzled glance Nathan threw John and wanted to grin. But he held it in. As the third man in the group, his was the most precarious position. In his case, it wasn't Nathan and John he needed to cater to, but Dana.

"I've got to go to the bathroom." Dana jumped up suddenly, dumping Kody's foot off the chair.

They all scrambled to their feet as manners dictated, and Kody grinned as he realized he wasn't the only one trying to hide a rock-hard bulge in his pants.

Well, at least the damned thing still works.

Chapter Nine

Dana splashed cold water on her face, but it did little to cool the fire in her pussy, a fire all three men seemed determined to fan. *Even worse, I enjoyed it.* The fleeting touches by Nathan and John seated on either side, along with their thick thighs brushing hers, had put her in a state of arousal that almost made her scream, *Take me now.* She could even picture it, the food and dishes flying as they laid her on the table and tore her clothes from her so they could take turns plowing between her thighs.

Dana sat down hard on the toilet, her knees too wobbly to support her. If it had been only Nathan and John teasing, she could have probably borne it. But Kody, stroking her with his foot—how decadent—had just about made her come. If someone would have told her a few days ago she'd allow a man to stroke her pussy with his foot at dinner, she would have laughed. Now, all she wanted was for him to finish what he'd started.

Dana squirmed, her panties soaking wet and her clit throbbing for relief. It crossed her mind that she should finish what they'd started while they waited. Returning while still so highly aroused, holding on to her morals and self-control by a thread, seemed like a bad idea.

Before she could change her mind, she unbuttoned her pants and shoved her hand down her undies.

She cupped herself and managed a cramped stroke of her clit. Her snug jeans held her legs too close together for her to masturbate properly, and the confinement frustrated her. Blushing, even as she couldn't stop herself, she shoved her pants and undies down around her ankles and sat back down on the closed toilet lid, spreading her thighs as far as she could.

I'll show them, she thought as she rubbed her swollen nub. She closed her eyes and couldn't prevent images of the guys from appearing. Nathan kissing her, dominating her mouth, while John sucked at her nipples. And as for Kody, the blond playboy, he'd be between her legs, his tongue lapping at her cream. The idea of all three of them pleasing her made her tremble. Her breathing hitched as she stroked herself faster, her erotic tension coiling quicker than she ever remembered.

A knock on the door, followed by Nathan saying, "Are you all right in there?" almost made her fall off the toilet seat. "Dana?" The handle rattled.

Dana jumped up, blushing red, even though she knew he couldn't see what she'd been doing. "Um, just a minute," she replied. She bit her cheek not to laugh at the ridiculous situation she found herself in. Even worse, she wanted to finish what she'd started. *He'd probably break down the door before I was done, though.* The idea excited her, though, as opposed to dousing her arousal. *I've completely lost my mind.*

She shuffled to the sink and turned on the water to scrub her hand, which smelt of pussy and would act like a billboard announcement to her bathroom endeavor if she didn't erase its scent before she returned to face the three werewolves with their enhanced sense of smell.

Who am I kidding? There's no way they could have missed the smell of me of getting horny at dinner. Sometimes being a werewolf sucked because it made hiding involuntary bodily reactions impossible. *But it doesn't mean I've changed my mind, no matter what my body thinks.* Her wolf stirred in her mind, reminding her of its feelings on the matter. *Fine, my wolf doesn't have a problem with the whole mating thing. But too bad. I'm the one in charge.*

Hands dried, she could still smell herself, smell the heat. She peered down at her crotch with a sigh. She grabbed some tissue, scrubbing her pussy to erase the signs of her arousal. Her vigorous rubbing, though, didn't help the situation. With a curse, she pulled up her pants, only to come in contact with her damp panties.

She wrinkled her nose. *Eew!* But with no

choice—because she sure as hell wasn't going to remove them—she bore it and buttoned her pants. She took one last peek in the mirror and almost didn't recognize herself. Her cheeks were flushed, her eyes bright and heavy-lidded. All in all she had an "I'm horny" look. Maybe they wouldn't notice.

With one last deep breath, she went back out and met Nathan's knowing grin.

"Everything okay in there?" he asked with an arched brow.

"Fine," she muttered, dropping her gaze.

"If you need help with *anything*, let me know. I'd be more than happy to oblige." He made his meaning clear, and annoyed at one of the causes of her confusion—and arousal—she slugged him in the stomach and left him gasping for air before returning to the dining area.

They'd cleared the table during her interrupted make-out session with herself and set it with a tray of evil-looking desserts, fluffy cream-filled pastries that screamed, *Eat me!*

Maybe I'll just have a bite of one before I go to my room.

John and Kody stood at her approach, and she bit her lip not to laugh as she noted them covering their groins. Out of fear or something else?

She sat down and immediately reached for a treat. She popped it into her mouth and bit down. She closed her eyes at the taste. Sweet, heavenly pleasure. The sugar melted on her tongue in a burst of flavor that made her groan. She savored it slowly and opened her eyes to grab another, but before she could move, she found three held out in front of her face.

Startled, she grabbed one and tried to curb her enthusiasm for the dessert, but it was hard, because not only did the second one taste just as freaking good, all three men were eyeing her with extreme hunger. She licked her lips clean and shivered when Nathan growled.

"What's your problem?" she asked.

His eyes glittered. "Stop teasing."

She frowned. "I'm just eating the dessert."

John cleared his throat, drawing her attention. "I think what he means to say—"

"Is you are one freaking hot lady," interrupted Kody with green eyes that glowed with interest.

"When you eat that, all I can think of is you eating my—"

He never did finish his sentence because Nathan dove over the table and hit Kody, taking them both to the floor. Dana watched them tussling on the floor with her mouth open.

"What the fuck are they doing?" she exclaimed.

"Training exercise to work off dinner," John replied, helping her from her seat. "Ignore them."

"I intend to. Boys," she said with a disgusted snort.

John linked her arm in his and led her away from the grunts and smacks of the fight, but she couldn't help craning back to watch.

John tried to divert her attention. "I think you should get some rest. It's been a long day, and you're still recovering."

Dana almost said, *I'm fine*, but kept her mouth shut, the words caught in her throat because, in the midst of the impromptu battle, shirts were getting torn, and the sight went beyond decadent. Hot, muscled flesh rippled and strained as Nathan and Kody rolled about, straining and heaving against the other. It was wrong and childish of them, but it still brought on an excitement that made her nipples tighten and her cleft quiver.

She wanted to turn around and join them, naked, feel those heavy bodies pressed to hers and rolling around in a frenzy. With a gasp, she faced forward and almost dragged John in her hurry to escape before she made her mental image a reality.

She made a beeline for the room Nathan had put her in. John stayed glued to her side, which didn't helping the tingling arousal sweeping through her. The heat pouring from her was great enough that she didn't dare allow him to follow her in. His calming presence was not working in the face of her body's erotic longing, and her body begged her to try to see if it could make him lose that steady demeanor. She whirled at the door and, with a bright smile, said, "Thanks. Dinner and dessert were great. See you in the morning."

John's eyes glinted with humor, and his lips tilted in a half-smile. When she would have fled, he gripped her about the waist. "Hold on a second. It's my turn to say good night."

He leaned in and brushed his lips across hers, a light touch that would have almost been chaste if not for the erection pressing against her stomach. Dana kept her hands clenched at her side, her nails digging into her palms lest she forget herself.

"Sweet dreams," he whispered against her mouth before letting her go.

Lips tingling, Dana tumbled into the bedroom and slammed the door shut. She leaned against the door and closed her eyes, trying to locate her control—a lost cause considering how they'd shredded it with their dinner foreplay.

Hot damn. I've never been so fucking horny in my life.

The thought of fleeing again briefly crossed her mind, but a quick glimpse out the window showed they'd placed a guard on patrol at the bottom of her previous escape route. She eyed the bedroom door, but she didn't figure she could flee past the three boys downstairs.

Nor was she entirely sure anymore that she wanted to run.

Being horny sure beats loneliness any day.

However, no matter her body's clamoring for satisfaction, it didn't mean she was ready yet to bind herself to them, but the idea was rapidly losing its repugnance. She couldn't deny her attraction to all three men, but could it just be hormones? What if she fucked them, allowed them to pleasure her?

Would she change her mind about staying after?

Somehow she didn't think a few orgasms would ever be enough.

* * * *

His hands caressed her, sliding down her body in a way that made her shiver and writhe. His large hand cupped her sex, and she arched against his palm.

"Please," she whispered.

Her lover, though, ignored her "please" and moved his touch back up to slide under her top to cup and squeeze her breasts. His mouth came down and sucked at her protruding nipple through the fabric. Then he bit down . . .

Dana's hold on the dream slipped. Her slow waking didn't stop the pleasurable sensations, though. She squirmed as the rough hands stroking up under her T-shirt made her skin burn and her nipples tighten. She gasped at the hot kiss placed at the base of her neck. Those same lips moved upward and caught hers in a torrid embrace that left her panting. She vaguely wondered, as she opened her mouth to a sinuous tongue, if perhaps she dreamt still.

"Oh, Dana."

The gruffly whispered words against her mouth made her open her eyes. "Nathan?" she murmured against the mouth that traced the outline of hers.

He grunted in reply, his lips moving sideways to find the lobe of her ear and nipping it. Dana, still half asleep, fought the sensual languor invading her body—a battle she was quickly losing and without a fight. His hands under her shirt cupped her breasts, and he stroked his thumbs over the erect tips. Dana sucked in a breath and arched. For a moment she couldn't speak, too caught up in the sensations he provoked. His pinch of her nubs sent a jolt of pleasurable pain that shot right to her pussy. It also helped her find her voice.

"What are you doing here?" she whispered, her hands twining in his hair instead of pushing him away like she knew she should.

"It's my bed," he replied before bringing his mouth back to hers. She allowed him to kiss her, reveled in the familiar and yet different feeling of his mouth on hers, his immature embraces of their youth now much harder and sensual in nature. Her body burned as arousal ignited all her nerve endings. Cream pooled in her cleft, aching for something to ease it. As if sensing her desire, he slid one hand down and, like in her dream, cupped her sex.

Still horny from earlier, she could only moan as he rubbed her. A part of her knew she should stop him, protest his taking advantage of her. But instead, she bucked as his fingers slipped under the fabric covering her cleft and he stroked her clit.

She could only hold tight to his shoulders as he circled her nub, teasing touches that had her gasping. His mouth bent and caught a nipple through her sleep shirt. He sucked it while his fingers delved between her moist folds and plunged into her channel.

Dana came. She bit her lip so as to hold back the scream as her orgasm tore through her body and left her trembling. Her shudders hadn't stopped when Nathan withdrew his fingers and rolled his much bigger body onto hers, bracing his weight on his forearms. He inserted a leg between her thighs and rubbed it against her mound. For a moment she allowed herself to enjoy it and pushed her pelvis back against him for the welcome friction against her pussy. Even though she'd climaxed, her body yearned for more, to feel his big cock claiming her.

But Dana was no wanton, even if she'd temporarily lost her mind. She also had too many things still to sort through without complicating matters with sex—even if that sex would be scorching and satisfying. Bad enough she'd allowed him to fondle her. "Stop," she panted.

"Why?" He resumed his pressure against her sex, and her fingers dug into his shoulders at the pleasure of it.

However, she well knew pleasure was fleeting, and she fought his erotic onslaught. "You need to stop because I don't know if I want this." Not entirely true. Her body definitely wanted what he offered. Her heart, however, still sat on the fence.

He paused and inhaled. "I can smell you do."

"Arousing my body isn't the same as convincing my mind," she retorted, his chauvinistic attitude making it easier to assert herself.

"But I want you," he replied, nudging her again with his erection.

"Not my problem."

"Easy for you to say," he grumbled. "You got your pleasure."

Dana shoved at him, his implacable weight not budging. "You took advantage of me while I was sleeping. You and I both know had you tried that while I was awake, you'd have ended up with a throbbing dick for an entirely other reason."

Nathan sighed and rolled off. "Are you still mad at me? I've said I was sorry about the past. I love you, Dana. I never stopped, and I went through hell these last twelve years waiting to find you again."

"A hell you brought on yourself," she snapped. The blame he laid at her feet doused the last of her ardor and roused her anger.

"So how long are you going to hold a grudge?"

"Forever at this rate. You can't expect to waltz back into my life and just resume where we left off."

"You wouldn't have a life if I hadn't saved it," he growled.

"And I thank you for your timely intervention." Without his rescue, she shuddered to think what would have happened.

"I'd rather you thanked me a different way." He left no doubt as to his meaning.

Isn't that just like a man to assume he should get payment for doing the right thing?

"God. You men are all such pigs. Me! Me! Me!" she yelled, sitting up so she could properly glare at him. "Did it ever occur to you for one freaking second that maybe I should get a say in this? What about what I want? Doesn't that count?"

"Of course it does, but—"

"See, there you go again. There is no 'but.' I want the freedom to make my own choices."

"So you can choose John," he said in a nasty tone.

"No. So I can do what's right for me. If John is right, then yes." At Nathan's snarl, she tempered her words. "If you're what I need, then I'll choose you. If it turns out I need both, or even three of you, then that's fine, but I want to make that choice. Me. Not you, your dick, and your stupid pack laws."

She expected him to yell at her, argue, maybe even hit her, given she didn't fully know the man he'd grown into. But he surprised her.

"I love you, Dana." He said the words quietly, and she could read the sincerity in his tone.

She laid her hand on his chest, the heat of his bare skin scorching, the steady thumping of his heart reverberating against her hand. "I know you do. And truthfully, I still love you too, or at least my memory of the boy I once knew. But"—she held up a hand to forestall him—"a teenage infatuation isn't a reason to join myself to you for the rest of my life. And neither are hormones. I need time to come to grips with everything that's happened. Time to figure out what's best for me. Please, can you do that for me?"

"I'd do anything for you."

Dana smiled, if tremulously. Tears clung to her lashes, and for a moment, she almost forgot her own plea, the urge to throw herself into his arms almost overwhelming. But that would be a mistake, and this time, she wanted to do things right.

"Thank you for understanding, Nathan. I really appreciate that. I guess I'll see you in the morning."

"Night, Dana." Nathan rolled onto his side and pulled the sheet up over his shoulder.

Dana gaped at his back. "Um, Nathan?"

"Yes?"

"What are you doing?"

"Trying to sleep. It is my bed, after all."

Dana's ire exploded. *Stupid fucking jerk. He just doesn't get it.* Grabbing her pillow, she hopped out of the bed.

"Where are you going?" he asked, sitting up.

"To find another bed," she snarled.

"There aren't any empty ones," he warned.

Dana whipped her pillow to the floor and lay down on the carpet, curling her legs up to her chest and hugging them.

Nathan sighed. She heard the mattress springs squeak a moment before strong hands scooped her up and deposited her back on the bed.

"Stubborn little minx. Take the bed. I'll sleep elsewhere."

He tucked the blanket around her, and

Dana, feeling contrite, said, "Kiss me good night."

He did so quickly, as if afraid she'd change her mind. His hard lips clung to hers for a heart-stopping moment.

"I don't suppose you'd change your mind?" he asked gruffly.

"Nice try," she sassed with a smile.

"See you in the morning."

Nathan left, and Dana snuggled into her sheets. His good-night embrace had reawakened some of her desire, and she wrapped the warmth of it around her as she allowed herself to imagine experiencing it every night. To give Nathan what he wanted—her. To sleep spooned in his arms, taking the love he had to give, and finally returning the emotions she'd bottled for so long.

But he wasn't the only one she wanted that with.

Her thoughts strayed to another man who gave her a different kind of peace in his presence. *John.* There wasn't the emotional baggage with John that she shared with Nathan, and she enjoyed that about him. She enjoyed how he made her feel, along with his calming presence that masked how he could set her on fire in a moment with just a brush of his lips.

And then there was the gorgeous Kody. His dancing green eyes and mischievous smile made her want to run and play like she hadn't since childhood.

Three very different men, and yet she found herself drawn to all of them. If someone were to force the decision on her right this second and said, *Choose one*, she'd find herself hard-pressed.

Fuck me, I don't understand why this is happening, but I want them all.

Chapter Ten

John hadn't slept much, his mind too consumed with thoughts of Dana. He'd heard Dana's fight with Nathan the previous night. How could he not with his enhanced werewolf hearing? He'd waited with bated breath to see if Nathan's plan to seduce her would work, but Dana prevailed and, with her plea to give her time and a choice, broke his heart.

John heard the hurt in her tone, the confusion as she struggled to sort through her emotions. He didn't consider it self-centered to admit he knew he played a part in her turmoil. It was evident to anyone with half a brain. Dana struggled with what her body and wolf wanted and what she, the woman, needed. Raised in a dysfunctional household, how could she not fight what they proposed?

The true wonder to John was the fact that she even contemplated it.

The gentlemanly thing to do would involve walking away and allowing her to make a choice without influence. That, however, required a selflessness that John discovered he didn't possess. He wanted Dana, and while he wouldn't force her, he also wouldn't just step aside and allow her to forget his interest. And with Nathan striking out with his heavy-handed tactics and scaring her in the process, he needed to step his seduction up a bit to show her a better alternative to flight. John didn't kid himself. He could see it in her eyes—Dana still hadn't decided if she should stay or go.

Given her probable angst this morning, John decided not to wait for a moment or for fate to intervene. He created his opportunity and snuck into her room, which wasn't as simple as it sounded. Nathan had spent the night on the floor in front of her door after she kicked him out while Kody had bunked down in the bushes outside her window. With her two exits covered, it was John who had resigned himself to a good night's sleep the evening previous—not that his plan to rest worked with his mind working overtime. He'd tried, though, knowing he'd require all his wits about him to deal with not only her but his pack brothers. The situation called for a delicate dance through emotions and jealousy where one misstep could signal disaster.

John bided his time. When Nathan staggered off with stretching and creaking limbs to the bathroom, John used the opportunity to slide into her room. He still didn't know what he would do or say as he approached the bed on silent feet, the lump in the middle not moving—at all. With only that as his warning, he managed to brace himself when his feet ended up swept out from under him.

He hit the floor hands-first and scissored his legs around to catch her before she could flee. It took some fast moving, but he maneuvered himself to act as a landing pad for her. She crashed into his body with a startled squeak. For good measure, John wrapped his arms tight around her and then grinned. "Morning, Dana."

She tried to look angry, but he could see the struggle. So he kissed the tip of her nose.

She giggled and relaxed on top of him. "Damned werewolves and their super senses."

"Don't tell me you actually thought you could flee?"

She shrugged and bit her lip. "Not really, but a girl's got to try. Am I in trouble?"

"Not in the least. Actually, I'm kind of happy you're determined to keep my skills honed. A man should always be on his toes in case of danger."

Her lips tilted in a smile that made his heart do a somersault. "And am I dangerous?"

"Most definitely. But I like it," he said with return grin. "Actually, I like a lot of things about you."

When she ducked her face under his chin, her warm breath feathering his neck, his already interested cock turned rock solid. It took more strength of will than he would have imagined to resist pressing himself against her. He tried to change the direction of his thoughts. "How are you feeling this morning?"

She lifted her head and peeked at him, exhibiting a girly coyness that seemed at odds with her usual tough bravado. He wondered if she was putting on an act for him to lull his senses or if she felt comfortable enough around him to drop her tough-girl façade. Only time and actions would tell, he guessed.

"I feel great. The soreness in my ribs is gone, and the last of the bruises seem to have faded overnight."

"Excellent. Although, I'll admit, I'm going to miss catering to my favorite patient."

"Ha!" she scoffed. "Anyone ever tell you that you're an ass kisser?"

"No, but I could be," he replied with a leer.

She laughed again, the sound like music to his ears. When she stopped, in the sudden silence, her stomach growled, and she blushed endearingly. John lost the battle with himself. He brushed her lips with his, a soft embrace that lasted only a fleeting moment but made him want to forget good manners and flip her over, tear off her clothes, and plow her sweet pussy.

"I guess we should get you downstairs so we can feed you," he said, his voice low.

He let his arms fall to the side, mentally urging her to move before he took advantage of her like his cock demanded. To his surprise, she didn't immediately move off him.

She stared down instead, a look of puzzlement creasing her brow. "I don't get you. I can feel you're happy to see me." She ground her hips against him in a delicious way that made his eyes almost roll up in his head. "And yet, you don't push me or even try to cop a feel or a real kiss. Why? I thought you wanted me. Or was I mistaken?"

John raised a hand and ran a finger down the side of her face, enjoying the softness of her skin but even more the way she tilted her head against his hand. "No mistake. I want you. I want to lick every inch of you and then make love to you until you scream my name." He swallowed hard when her eyes dilated and her lips parted on a breathy sigh. He allowed himself only one chaste kiss before continuing. "I want to claim you as my mate and raise pups with you. But I told you. I won't force you. When you decide you're ready, I'll be here, ready to love you silly. If you want my mark, I will give it to you gladly. But you make the choice. You decide when."

His words mirrored the ones she'd said to Nathan the previous night, but he intended no subterfuge. He meant them. He wouldn't force himself on her if she was unwilling.

They'd both end up miserable otherwise.

Besides, if he was right about her, she'd eventually come to him. He just had to survive the wait.

He could see he'd stunned her, and then the most wondrous thing happened. She leaned forward and pressed her mouth to his, a fleeting embrace, but one freely given. "Thank you," she whispered.

Then she kissed him again, deeply, her lips sliding over his in a way that made him tremble to control himself from doing what both his wolf and body demanded. *Claim her. Mark her. Make her ours.* John clenched his fists to his sides, not trusting himself to even hug her. He let her set the pace of the kiss, which ended too soon—not soon enough.

She got off him and stood up. John could only lie there stunned. He gazed up at her with what was surely a hungry look. Her eyes also appeared bright, and he could scent her arousal. With an impish grin, she offered him her hand, which was how Nathan found them when he walked in.

Nathan's brows beetled together, and John waited for him to say something stupid and jealous, but he held his tongue. "Breakfast is ready," he announced curtly and turned on his heel to march out.

Dana sighed. "For a man who used to be okay with the idea of sharing me, he's gotten awfully jealous."

"Nathan is scared of losing you. That you'll turn to one of us alone and leave him out in the cold."

"If he keeps up that attitude, it is a definite possibility," she grumbled.

John slapped her on the ass. "Behave. Just like you, Nathan's working through some heavy emotional shit. Give him a break." John held out his arm and bit back a smile of satisfaction as she linked hers in it. Baby steps. "Let's go feed you. We've got a busy day ahead. Nathan wants to show you the compound and all the changes he's made."

"I'd like that. And what are your plans?" she asked, not looking at him.

John smiled at her roundabout way of asking if she'd see him. "I'm going to be with you, of course. Unless you'd prefer I stay behind."

Her hand squeezed his arm. "I'd like it if you came, too."

They went downstairs and found Nathan making breakfast while Kody poured the juice.

"Morning, darling," Kody said with a wink. "I hope you slept like crap all by yourself."

Dana sucked in a breath and laughed. "You are incorrigible."

"Yes, yes I am," Kody replied in a deadpan tone. John saw the twinkle in his eye and waited for him to get even more outrageous. "Anytime you want to correct me, let me know. I'd bend over gladly for you."

John laughed at the look on Dana's face. Even Nathan ruefully chuckled.

"Sit down and shut up, Kody, before I bend you over for my belt instead of her hand," Nathan threatened, but with a smile.

Dana shook her head at their banter, but the laughter ended up a good start for the day, and breakfast went by with ease.

After breakfast, Kody announced he had to run into town for supplies, and Dana, with a pointed look at Nathan, said she'd write him a list of things she required since she hadn't been given time to pack.

The compound was comprised of a gated community with family homes, a rec center, and a basic corner store. Groceries and other staples required a drive of about forty-five minutes into town. But these things did require funds. To earn a paycheck, some of the males worked in the nearby environs, but given the size of most families, a lot of the wolves went for employment that gave them time away, trucking being the most prevalent. Truckers could be gone from one day to several weeks at a time, so it eased sometimes crowded living conditions and gave the females breathing room. Given the multi-mate status of most families, the females had no need to work, although some of the older ones whose pups had progressed to school age chose to do so to combat boredom.

As pack alpha, Nathan didn't have a job per se, not that he needed one. A great-great-grandfather of his had done well financially and invested his earnings. Nathan maintained those accounts, somewhat depleted during his father's tenure, and had managed to add to them by doing odd jobs for the Lycan council. Mostly rogue hunting, a dirty, dangerous job that paid quite lucratively, especially in recent years with the increase in rogues. Thinking of those miscreants made John vaguely wonder if Nathan had obtained any leads on the whereabouts of the remaining shifters who'd abducted and abused Dana. The rogues' rabid behavior needed addressing, and John hoped to be a part of the group that meted out their punishment.

John waited in the living room with Nathan for Dana to finish with her list.

"I don't suppose I could ask you to stay away from her?" Nathan asked in a quiet voice.

John looked over at him. "Nope. I know what she means to you, Nathan. I won't keep her to myself if that's what you're afraid of. You and I both know that if you want to avoid troubles with the Lycan council, it would be best if she ends up mating with all of us."

"I've wanted and chased after her for so long that the idea of sharing just isn't sitting well," Nathan admitted.

"I'd quote pack law to you, but you already know it. You know the Lycan council won't turn a blind eye to anyone flaunting that law, not given the low birth rates we've been experiencing. Even if it weren't for pack law, I wouldn't back off. She calls to me and my wolf. I can't stop thinking about her." *And wanting her.* John kept that part to himself.

"Do me a favor and give me a chance to claim her first. I realize that to keep her, I'm going to have to share. It's funny because, twelve years ago, the roles were reversed, with me wanting it and her vehemently opposed. I'll get over it. I have to if I'm going to keep her and stay with the pack. In a sense, I'm glad it's going to be with you and Kody instead of some of the others in the pack."

Nathan's honesty and the difficult truths he admitted out loud touched John. "Things will work out, Nathan. Now keep in mind, though, I can't promise you'll be first marked. The choice is Dana's. But I won't pursue her hard until you've given it your best shot."

"Fair enough," Nathan agreed.

"Once you've marked her, though, all bets are off. I will woo her."

"Understood. But do me a favor," Nathan said, turning to him with a half-smile. "If she really has done a one-eighty and decides to take us all to bed at once, keep your dick away from my ass."

John gaped at him and then laughed. "Make sure you keep yours pointed in her direction and you've got a deal." He held his hand out, and Nathan gripped it tight.

Dana took that moment to come down the stairs, and she eyed them oddly, probably because they couldn't stop snickering.

"What's so funny?"

Nathan stared at the ceiling, a ruddy color suffusing his face. John covered for him. "Just wagering if Kody's going to be able to buy those feminine products you asked for or if he's going chicken out."

Dana smiled wickedly. "Actually, he says they won't be a problem at all, especially once I told him he'd also get to pick me up some underwear since Nathan forbade me from leaving the compound."

Nathan shifted uncomfortably. "Only until you've mated with us. I'm still not convinced you won't flee."

"Smart wolf," Dana sassed. She patted him on the cheek and, with a smirk, sauntered out the front door.

Nathan stared after her, stunned, while John just laughed again.

She's just what we need to keep us in line.

Chapter Eleven

Once outside, Dana found herself caught between John and Nathan, a place she didn't want to flee. Although she did want to strip in an attempt to cool down. With an alpha on one side and a man who could have been alpha had but ended up beta on the other, they formed an impressive wall of male flesh. As they strode with her through the vastly changed compound, their bodies brushed hers—a hard thigh against her hip, a hand to guide in the middle of her back or on her waist, the occasional whisper in her ear that tickled. Talk about a smorgasbord of sensations. Within an hour, her body aroused, her nerves shot, she seesawed between an urge to scream and ripping off her clothes in an open invitation to claim her. Her mind leaned toward the second scenario, which wetted her panties even further.

She controlled herself—barely. She tried to focus on what they showed her, from the solar panels and wind turbines that provided all their electrical needs to the composting and garden areas. But while she noted all the eco-friendly changes and increased number of homes, she just couldn't concentrate. Every so often familiar faces would come up to say hello, and she'd snap out of her self-imposed torture to exchange hellos and hugs. But all too soon, they'd pass on, and she'd return to her coiled state of sexual readiness. After a while, even her state of mind couldn't hide the fact that she noticed more new faces than old. Needing distraction, she asked Nathan about it.

"Is it me, or is there a lot of new blood here now?"

"You'd be correct," Nathan replied, stopping to sit on a bench in a common park area. John sat beside him, and Dana eyed the few inches left between them and knew she wouldn't fit—although she did, for one hot moment, wonder how it would feel to squash herself between them, naked of course.

She took a step back, and as if realizing her dilemma, Nathan snagged her around the waist and settled her on his lap, where her bottom rubbed against a hardness that left no doubt about his happiness about having her sitting on him. Dana glanced over to John, uncomfortable at this familiar and intimate gesture in front of another man who interested her, but John met her worried look with a gentle smile and nod.

Dana relaxed at his acceptance and barely noticed another brick coming down in her wall of resistance toward the whole multi-mate thing.

"The new people are the Lycan council's doing. They noticed an increase in birth defects and mental instability. They blamed it on too much pack inbreeding. They requested packs join an exchange program."

"And the packs went for it?" That surprised her. Packs tended to live isolated lives. While ruled by a Lycan council, who dealt with keeping them out of the public eye and disputes between packs, outside of that, packs ruled themselves.

"At first, there was some chafing, mostly by the alphas and the old-timers. The young ones, though, saw it as an opportunity for change and jumped on it."

"I'm surprised your dad allowed it." After her dad, Nathan's dad was the biggest prick she'd ever met.

"He didn't. After you left, things went downhill in the pack," Nathan started. "My dad went from bully to complete asshole. I escaped a lot of his abuse and excesses going to college, but when I returned for visits, I couldn't ignore how everyone was living in a state of fear. We ended up losing some of the good families during that time. They snuck out and went to the council for pack reassignment. This went on for a few years, with my dad getting more and more paranoid. He was convinced the humans were on to us and would end up killing us all."

"Why the hell would he think that?" It

sounded bad of her, but humans of this generation were oblivious.

"He had reason for his madness. Males from the pack were disappearing."

That got her attention. "What? They ran away?"

"Nope. Some we found, torn to pieces. Others ended up resurfacing as part of rogue packs."

"I thought rogue packs were rare." Anybody who refused to follow council law was declared rogue and hunted to the death. The council protected the Lycans ruthlessly, and any wolves who didn't toe the line were destroyed for the greater good of the packs.

"They used to be rare, but not anymore. The Lycan council has been looking into it, and while we know the number of rogues has increased, we have yet to figure out the reason why. Some of those who defected were married, and seemingly happy."

"Has anyone talked to them?" Dana's brow creased.

Nathan's eyes stared off into the distance, the sorrow in them all too clear. "We've caught several, one from this pack even."

"And?" she pressed when he went silent.

"They're mad," John replied softly when Nathan didn't.

"Mad at what?"

"Not mad as in angry," John corrected.

"I mean their minds are warped. Their reasoning skewed."

"But how? Did they catch some sickness?"

Nathan shrugged. "That's what the council wants to find out. It's also why we increased the security around this place. Along with the electrical and barbed fence around the compound, we have motion sensors, cameras, and guards patrolling the perimeter in groups of two. Folks go out in groups after dusk or not at all."

"That's nuts."

"Maybe," Nathan replied with a sigh, "but since our new preventative measures, we've managed to halt the disappearances."

She suddenly thought of Kody. "Hold on a second. You let Kody leave by himself. How do you know he'll be safe?"

"Oddly enough, they only strike at night. Once nightfall hits, no one leaves the compound alone."

Dana suddenly had a vivid image of her pockmarked abductor and shivered. "Those wolves who caught me, they were rogues, weren't they?"

"Yes. The Lycan council received numerous reports about their misdemeanors and put out a decree for their elimination. They contacted me about taking care of the problem around the same time we got the report on your location."

She ignored the first part to latch onto the second. "You were spying on me?" she asked.

"Searching for," Nathan corrected. "It wasn't the first time we'd gone to get you, only to end up empty-handed."

Dana smiled smugly. "That's because I was good at hiding."

Nathan squeezed his arms around her. "I caught you in the end."

"And thank God we arrived when we did," John added.

The somber reminder killed her humor. "Did you kill all the bastards who took me?" She'd avoided thinking about that since her recovery but now had a burning need to know.

"Most. Don't worry. They can't get to you here."

Nathan left unsaid, *You're safe with us,* but she heard it in his voice and saw it in John's eyes. *Safety, just one more reason to stay. If I let them mark me, I wouldn't have to worry about other wolves trying to claim me anymore. No more setting booby traps and looking over my shoulder. No more starting over. No more sleeping alone.* That, more than anything, appealed to her. Another brick of resolve crumbled. In truth, the wall she'd erected around her emotions and reasons had a hole big enough to drive a truck full of wolves through, three in particular. *I think I want to do this. No, I know I want to do this.* She kept her decision to herself. Now, whilst discussing somber things, wasn't the time. She'd wait until later, when she got Nathan alone. He should be the first she marked and claimed because, after all, she'd loved him the longest.

"Penny for your thoughts?" Nathan prodded.

Startled, she blurted out the first thing that came to mind, other than stripping him and seeing the joy on his face when she told him to take her. "So you never finished telling me what happened to your dad."

Nathan sighed. "It's not pretty. He kidnapped a human from town then tortured and killed him."

"Why?"

"Who the hell knows." He shrugged. "When the pack found out, I had no choice. I challenged him for control of the pack."

"You killed your father?" The news shocked her, mostly because of the devastation to Nathan. Hating one's parent was one thing, having to end their life another.

Nathan's eyes clouded over. "No, but I might as well have. I fought him and won. But because of what he'd done, I had to hand him over to the council as my first act as alpha. The council executed him for his crimes."

"Oh, Nathan, I'm so sorry," she exclaimed, and on impulse, she threw her arms around his neck. She hugged him tight, horrified at what he'd done but, at the same time, recognizing the need. When a wolf went bad, especially an alpha in a position of power, he needed removal. It just sucked the bad apple happened to be his father.

She turned her head sideways on Nathan's shoulder and saw John watching them. For a moment guilt filled her. How could it not when she was plastered to one man she wanted while the other she longed for watched? But she saw no jealousy in John's eyes, just a calm acceptance and approval.

Nathan might end up first, but you'll be a close second. She found herself giddy at the thought of making both these men hers.

A feminine "There you are" had her straightening and hopping off Nathan's lap. She flushed at the intimate position she'd gotten caught in. Lycans were open about such things, but she'd spent many years among the humans with their more prudish natures.

A voluptuous beauty strolled toward them, sex appeal oozing from her hourglass figure encased in skintight jeans and a skimpy tank top.

"John and Nathan, just the big, strong men I was looking for."

Dana gnashed her teeth at the syrupy sweetness in her voice. *Slut.*

"What's up, Melinda?" Nathan asked.

"I need to borrow you both for a little bit. My men are out of town, and I need some stuff moved."

The redhead's smile made Dana's jaw tighten. *Is this bitch seriously hitting on my men? In front of me?*

"Can't you find someone else to help you?" Nathan asked, getting up to stand behind Dana.

"It'll just take a moment."

Dana had heard enough. "I don't think so."

"Excuse me?" Melinda looked her up and down with a haughty sneer. "And who are you to speak for them?"

"I am their promised mate, and I say you won't be borrowing them. If you need furniture moved, plumbing fixed, or anything else, open the Yellow Pages and find a professional."

"You can't speak to me like that," Melinda snarled, narrowing her eyes and taking an aggressive step forward.

Dana growled back and let her wolf rise as she met the woman, toe to toe, glare for glare. "Consider this your last warning."

"Bitch," spat Melinda. "I'll show you to speak to me like that."

Melinda went to grab Dana's hair, and Dana gave a low chuckle as she avoided the redhead's flailing hands and, in a quick move, swept her feet from under her, sending the slut to the ground. Dana knelt on her chest.

"Submit," Dana warned, cocking and pulling her fist back.

"Nathan, you're not going to let this outsider talk to me like that, are you?"

"As my future wife, she can and will talk to you any way she likes. Especially if you're going to act like a bitch in heat. Now I suggest you call your mates and tell them to come home if you're that lonely," Nathan ordered. "And if I hear of you harassing any of the other husbands in the compound, you'll be asked to leave. We don't condone cheating."

Dana smirked as she got up off the redhead. Melinda's face turned a blotchy red, and she staggered to her feet and stalked away.

Dana resisted an urge to stick her tongue out at her.

"Future mates, eh?" Nathan sounded pleased.

But now embarrassed over her very jealous reaction, Dana snapped, "Maybe. I haven't completely decided. I like the way you both sat back and let her try to attack me. What happened to protecting me?" She placed her hands on her hips and glared at them.

Nathan grinned. "What, and miss you putting her in her place?"

"Please. Anybody with half a brain could see you'd kick her ass," John added.

Finding herself somewhat mollified,

Dana's lips twitched. "True. I guess you're forgiven for now."

"So did you mean what you said, though? Have you decided?" Nathan eyed her anxiously, and she could see equal interest in John's eyes.

"That's for me to know and you to find out," she challenged. Then she took off running.

* * * *

Nathan's heart stuttered at her declaration. *Is she finally ready to let me claim her?*

"You go after her. I'll meet you back at the house," John said. "Good luck."

"Thanks, man." Nathan gave his friend a respectful nod but didn't linger. He had a feisty woman to catch. *Mine.* Nathan took off after Dana and had to work to keep up because she ran like the wind even on two legs. She gave no warning about her intention to shift. One moment, she sprinted. The next, clothing burst from her in tatters, and a golden wolf went bounding off into the woods that were a part of the compound.

Damn, she's gotten fucking good at shifting. Considering she'd lived alone for the last twelve years, she'd mastered her wolf side better than those who'd lived with it a lifetime. Nathan followed suit, his clothes shredding as his muscles thickened and his bones reshaped. He landed on four paws, his senses even more acute, and continued to give chase.

He thanked the fact that they were finally alone. Maybe now he could plead his case with her or, even better, show her without words how he felt. He followed Dana through the woods, the exhilaration of the hunt making his blood pump. The towering trees shaded them from the sunlight, but enough filtered through the branches to lift the shadows.

The pack had managed to corral over two hundred acres in order to provide a safe running ground. Not the ideal solution for a species used to racing miles when the moon madness hit, but at least they needn't fear casualties from the rogues. The forest ringed around the houses in the compound with a cleared strip between it and the electrified fence.

As he bounded over the fallen logs and stirred up the dead leaves, he thought over Dana's claim she was his future mate. He'd prayed and hoped for this day, and now that it appeared on nigh, he didn't want anything to fuck it up. So long as he was her first, he could handle the rest. And, besides, now that he'd readjusted himself to the mind-set of sharing, he could admit that the idea titillated him.

One step at a time. First I need to mark her then, along with my pack brothers, show her how it could be.

His enhanced sight saw Dana, in the

distance ahead, burst free from the forest cover, and worried she might have forgotten his warning about the fence, he poured on the speed and shot out of the woods and stumbled in shock. He yelped as he lost his footing and rolled in a tangle of limbs. He landed muzzle-first on the ground.

Her laughter bathed him as he shifted back to his human form and glared up at her in mock anger. Who could retain any ire—or sense, for that matter—with her standing, glorious and beautiful, in all her naked glory in front of the fence?

"What happened to your modesty?" he grumbled. The Dana he remembered had a thing about nudity in front of others, even him.

She grinned at him saucily and planted her hands on her hips, drawing his eyes from her face to the body she proudly displayed. "If you've got it, flaunt it."

And she did have it. Nathan drank in the sight of her breasts, full and perky with light rose-colored nipples that puckered as he watched. His cock rose as he further perused her from her indented waist to her flaring hips and the curls that hid her woman's core which even while hidden, couldn't mask the scent of her arousal.

"Dana." He took a step forward, and the cocky woman disappeared for a moment, hidden behind the girl he remembered who chewed her lip in uncertainty. She whirled from him and gestured with her arms to the fence.

"Holy shit. You weren't kidding about the fence. This must have cost a fortune to put in. How the hell did you get the local human government to agree?"

Nathan didn't want to talk. He was more interested in the view of her heart-shaped ass and wondering how it would look bent over. She threw him a look over his shoulder as she waited for his answer.

"The mayor for the township is a dormant male from the pack. He pushed it through, claiming we needed it for protection from wildlife."

The irony wasn't lost on her. "That's hilarious."

When Dana kept studying the fence, instead of facing him, Nathan took the steps that separated them and folded her into his arms, drawing her back into his body. She stiffened at first then relaxed.

Nathan rubbed his face against the top of her head, breathing in her fragrance while his cock pushed hotly against her back. Her body trembled slightly.

"Is it stupid to be scared?" she whispered.

"Don't be. I won't let anyone hurt you ever again."

"I wasn't talking about rogues. I'm scared

of the whole mating thing. Scared that I'll tie myself to you, the others, and wake up and realize it was the wrong decision. That I'll get hurt or end up miserable like my mom."

"You don't have to choose us all."

"But the pack law—"

"Screw it. I lost you once over it. I won't let it happen again."

She turned in his arms and peered up at him. "You'd defy the council's laws for me?"

"I would." And he meant it. The blinders of youth were gone. He'd achieved everything he wanted, but without the woman he loved, it meant nothing. He was nothing.

"And if I choose to mate with others and obey the law?" she asked tentatively, staring at a spot on his bare chest.

"Then I'll share you. I ask only one thing, though."

"What?"

"Mark me first. Let me be the first to claim you."

Dana peered up at him and smiled. "I think that could be arranged, although you do realize that it's not the order of marriage that decides the dominant male in the relationship?"

The lead mate in a polyamorous grouping went by dominance. As alpha, Nathan, no matter what order he was marked, would end up lead mate.

"I know. But I want to be the first to call

you mine. The first to make you cry out in pleasure. The first to tell you I love you."

"Do you? I'm not the same girl you remember. I'm a lot more ruthless and violent than I used to be," she admitted ruefully.

"You call it ruthless. I see it as strength, the perfect attribute for the woman who will rule this pack at my side as mate and wife."

Her eyes brimmed, and she leaned up. Nathan bent to meet her, his lips claiming hers. The touch electrified him, and his already hard cock pulsed against her bare stomach. Her arms twined around his neck, hugging him to her tightly, and he returned her embrace, squeezing her nude body to his. The feel of her skin against his drove him mad with lust.

It's been so long . . . so long since he'd buried himself in her moist heat, the small taste of her passion the night before just a teaser. He dragged his lips from the sweetness of her mouth and down the column of her throat. She moaned as he nibbled her skin. He didn't linger. Too long had he dreamed of this moment. He let his tongue lead the way to her breasts, and he circled her nipple, teasing her so that she gasped. His hands cupped her bottom as he bent her back. He leaned over her and took a nipple into his mouth, sucking the shriveled berry. The smell of her arousal wafted up and made him groan.

He switched breasts, torturing her other

erect nub with his mouth and teeth, tugging on it and then sucking her globe into his mouth until she cried out and her fingers dug into his shoulders, her nails biting him in a way that made his desire rage fiercer.

With her bent backward and him folded over her, it was kind of awkward. He dropped to his knees and nuzzled her belly with his face. She clasped his hair.

His hands spanned her buttocks, and he squeezed them as he moved his face lower to rub against her pubes, letting her scent mark him.

Her thighs were clamped, and he pushed at their seam, parting them enough to flick his tongue out to touch her sex.

She moaned his name.

Encouraged by her response, he stroked her again. "Part your legs for me, baby." With trembling limbs, she did as told, and he ducked slightly under her to open his mouth wide over her damp lips.

She cried out, and her body buckled. He caught her with the hands on her buttocks and supported her as he tasted her. She was like honey on his tongue, and he lapped at her moist core while inhaling deeply of her fragrance, a musky aroma that made his cock strain and bob between his legs.

He found her clit with his lips and worked it, relentlessly flicking his tongue against it back and forth, spurred on by her tightening grip in his hair.

Her climax hit without warning. Dana wailed as she bucked in his grasp, but he held tight and plunged his tongue into her sex, enjoying the flexing of her muscles as she quivered her release.

The shocks in her body subsided, and with one last kiss to her cleft, Nathan went to his feet. He kept his arms around her and smiled in satisfaction as she gazed up at him with heavy lids.

"Wow," she whispered.

"It's not over," he promised, nudging her belly with his cock.

Her eyes widened, and a shiver went through her body.

He wanted to tell her to bend over, but at a rustling sound from the woods behind them, he instead positioned her behind him. He turned to face whomever approached.

A mottled wolf emerged from the forest, and Nathan sighed as he recognized Jeffrey.

Jeffrey changed, and before he spoke, Nathan knew his claiming of Dana would have to occur later.

"The council needs to speak with you."

"Race you back," Dana said before shifting behind him and springing forth with a yip.

Jeffrey watched her bound off and had

the decency to look chagrined. "Sorry. They said it was important, or I wouldn't have interrupted."

"I know. Did they say what it was about?"

Jeffrey shook his head. "Just that they needed to talk to you ASAP."

Nathan wondered what they wanted. Only one way to find out. "I better go because, if she beats me, I'll never hear the end of it."

But he'd underestimated Dana, for she beat him to the house and blew him a saucy kiss as she strode in, stark naked.

Nathan grinned, and his wolf yipped, the anticipation of the night exciting them. *It won't be long now until you're mine.*

Chapter Twelve

Dana ran up the stairs to her room, her brave immodesty of moments ago a sham to drive Nathan wild. *And it had worked.*

Twelve years of abstinence had turned her into an instant wanton it seemed. Now that her sexual floodgates had opened, she couldn't seem to stop the flow of emotions and desires swamping her. Nor did she want to. How she'd survived all those years in her sterile, lonely world she didn't know. She did, however, realize she could never go back, not if she ever wanted to find happiness.

And she had three men to thank for that, John with his calming presence and fleeting touches, Kody with his ribald humor and bold flirtation, and Nathan with his dominating presence and touch. Just remembering the way he'd pleasured her out in the open made her nipples tighten and her sex flood with moisture.

What a shame about the interruption. Seeing Nathan so aroused, because of her, made her want to go find him and drag him back to the room to continue what they had begun. But a quick glance at the clock showed the dinner hour approached, and she didn't want to shove it in John's and Kody's faces that she and Nathan had become intimate. Besides, she looked forward to seeing all of them.

The hot sex and marking that would signal the beginning of her new life as part of a pack again could wait until later. The anticipation was sure to be a titillating foreplay of its own.

She showered with a smile on her face, her hands slickly stroking her body as she recalled the afternoon's tryst. When she came out, horny as hell, she saw bags heaped on the bed, along with a lounging Kody.

Dana clutched her towel around her and cursed her straggly, damp hair state.

Kody grinned. "Hmm, wet, just the way I want you."

She blushed at his innuendo, but her body, already aroused, responded to his words with a quiver.

"I bought all the stuff you asked for," he said, gesturing to the bags. "I also picked you up a couple extra things, like a few dresses and shoes."

"Dresses? God, it's been a while since I've worn something other than pants." She'd had no reason to dress up or indulge in feminine articles.

"I'd prefer you naked, but there's something to be said about unwrapping." Kody flashed her a cocky grin.

Dana laughed. "What am I going to do with you?"

"Anything you want," he replied in a serious tone.

The intent look he tossed her way flustered her a bit. If it hadn't been for what she'd begun with Nathan, she would have flung off her towel and shown him what she wanted—him naked. *I am turning into a veritable slut.* And she couldn't care less.

Dana approached the bed and opened the nearest bag. She pulled out some light summer frocks, along with some sandals and scraps of material that made her gasp. "You bought me thongs!"

"Damned straight I did," Kody said with an unrepentant leer that went well with his twinkling green eyes. "And I'm hoping you'll wear one to dinner along with one of your new dresses 'cause, after my shower, I was planning on going barefoot." He waggled his brows at her, and Dana laughed at his audacity.

"You are so bad!"

"Funny, I was going to say I was *really good.*"

He came up off the bed so quickly Dana took a step back. He stood in front of her and stared down, not saying anything, but his intent was clear in his gaze. Dana's eyes fluttered shut as he leaned in and brushed her lips with his.

She moved in closer to him and parted her mouth in invitation. He didn't press his advantage. He tugged her lower lip between his and sucked it before letting it go and stepping back.

"See you at dinner," he whispered with bright eyes. "And thanks for not maiming me this time."

He began to walk toward the door. Dana whipped off her towel and yodeled, "Oh, Kody."

His head craned to look back. She licked a finger and ran it down her body. Then she winked and said, "I can't wait."

His eyes widened, and still in motion, he walked into the doorjamb. He bounced back and scowled at her, even as his lips tried to tug upward into a smile. "And they say I'm the bad one."

She blew him a kiss, which he caught with a grin before he closed the door.

Dana debated wearing her own clothes but, in the end, wore what Kody had chosen for her. She had to give him credit. The man had taste and an eye for size. The dress fit her perfectly and, while it hit her knee, clung to her figure in a flattering manner. She stepped into the flimsy panties, biting her lip at the strange sensation of the string-like part sliding up between her cheeks. Funny how a pair of undergarments could make her wet and cause her to blush. She ended up not wearing a bra. She liked the way her nipples protruded through the fabric when she tweaked them.

Tonight was about seduction and changing her life. Hopefully for the better.

Dana slipped on a pair of sandals but refrained from makeup. She wasn't into unnatural artifice, and her wolves didn't seem to mind. She dried and brushed her hair until it crackled and floated about her in a silken wave. She peered at herself in the mirror, stunned. Gone were the lines of tension in her forehead. Her cheeks held a pink flush. Her eyes glowed with brightness, and her lips appeared lush and full—like a woman who kept getting kissed.

Taking a deep breath, nervous at what she planned to do later on—namely exchange marks with Nathan—she left the room. She heard the murmur of the boys' voices as she approached the stairs, but as she descended, it got dead silent. She wondered if she'd managed to tuck her skirt into her undies or something given the way they regarded her with dropped jaws.

"What?" she asked when she reached the bottom and they still didn't say a word. She craned to peer behind her, but everything seemed in place.

John recovered first and approached her to grab her hand. "You look beautiful," he murmured. He drew her in for a chaste kiss, or at least that might have been his intention. She licked the seam of his lips and heard his breath hitch. She looked forward to the near future when she'd get to see her calm doctor lose his cool.

"Thanks," she murmured, her insides tingling at their brief touch.

Kody hip checked John aside and lifted her hand to place a kiss on the palm of it—with a bit of tongue. "You are delicious-looking," he added.

Heat pooled between her thighs, and she knew he caught the scent of her arousal when he winked. Dana blushed even hotter.

Nathan picked Kody up and moved him aside, which made her giggle. He then stared down at her with burning eyes.

"What, don't you have something to say?" she teased.

He didn't reply, just drew her up for a deep kiss that left her in no doubt he liked her look.

"Hey, are you going to let her breathe anytime soon because I think your dinner is burning," Kody announced.

Nathan let her go, reluctantly. "Later," he whispered.

Dana just bit her lip and nodded. As Nathan busied himself at the oven, she allowed John to seat her, his hands lingering at her back in a way that made her want to turn in his arms for another kiss.

"I trust you had a good workout," John asked, sitting beside her.

"Um, you could say that," Dana stammered

Kody sat across from her and smirked. "I can't wait to *work out* with you."

Dana stuck her tongue out at him, and Kody laughed. "Don't point that thing unless you're prepared to use it."

Dana almost replied with, *Who says I'm not?* but held back. Until she marked all three of them, and they her, she needed to tread carefully, especially around Nathan, who seemed determined that she partner with him first.

John's arm rested across the back of her chair, and his fingers tickled her nape, making her all too aware of him beside her. The heat in her body made her wish she could hurry through dinner to get to the main event with Nathan—and then tomorrow with John, and then the next day with Kody. A pity she couldn't just do them all at once.

Dana almost sank under the table at the thought. *Am I so horny that I'm ready to just jump in bed with all three of them just like that?* She looked around at them, each appealing in his own right, each determined to make her happy. *Actually, yes, yes I am.*

The best part about her decision to give

in to her nature—and listen to her wolf—was the inner peace. She wasn't doing this because she had to or because they were forcing her. Her decision to embark on a true mating came about because she wanted it.

And her body craved it.

Dinner ended up almost a repeat of the previous day's, with the exception that there was a lot less tension between the boys. However, the touches and smiles had the same arousal-heightening effect. Dana felt drunk with all the innocent stimulation, enough that she abstained from the wine they served. With her luck it would go straight to her crotch, and she'd end up on the table begging them to take her. She wanted her first time with each to be one-on-one and special, something she could later remember as the moment she'd chosen to link her fate with a man who made her happy. Kody, despite his earlier tease of playing with her, kept his feet to himself—how unfortunate. But she knew it was out of respect for Nathan and the fact that this was to be his night. Not that it stopped them from teasing her in other ways.

In an effort to clear her thoughts, she broached Nathan's ill-timed phone call of earlier. "So what did the council want?" she asked, taking a bite of the decadent pasta covered in cream sauce that Nathan had prepared for dinner, along with some toasted cheese baguette.

"Knowing we'd rescued you, they were curious to know if you'd been claimed yet."

"And you told them?" she urged.

"That you would do so when you felt the time was right."

Dana shot him a smile, pleased with his answer. "That doesn't sound so urgent to me."

Nathan shifted in his seat. "They also sent a warning that one of their trackers followed some rogues, possibly the same ones who captured you, into the area."

Dana froze, her fork held in midair. Fear sent icy fingers up her spine, and she bit back a whimper as the memory of the pain and despair they'd subjected her to came back to haunt her. She suffered the memory and fear only for a moment before her inner courage and the comforting presence of the men around her melted that temporary emotion. "Let me know when you're going hunting. I'd love to be part of the group that takes those slimeballs down."

She saw the boys exchange a look and wanted to roll her eyes at their transparency. Like she didn't know they'd attempt to keep her at home, where they thought it safe. *Men can be so predictable. I do have to admit it is kind of cute, not to mention nice, to know I've got someone, make that several someones, watching my back.*

Their conversation veered by design as they distracted her from the Lycan council's warning, but Dana made a mental note to pull out her pistol loaded with silver bullets from her duffel bag. From now on, she wasn't going anywhere without the weapon she called The Equalizer. Brute strength and testosterone were no match for a well-placed bullet.

Around dessert, relaxed if horny, she broached something that nagged at her. "I don't get it. How come none of you have girlfriends? I mean you're good-looking, young, and house-trained. You should have women lining up to leash you," she asked, suddenly wondering in horror if perhaps they'd begun to toy with her while stringing along some other poor girl. While female Lycans were prized as mates and not available for dallying, there were dormants and widows available, and even if human girls couldn't carry pups, they could sate a male's baser needs.

John replied first. "I haven't been with anyone in about two years now. I honestly just didn't have any interest. I must have known you were coming." He squeezed her thigh when he spoke.

Nathan and Kody both groaned at his cheesy line, but Dana smiled at him. Perhaps a tad corny. Yet she liked it.

"I never keep a regular girlfriend," Kody boasted. "I don't need to because, everywhere I go, women fall all over me." Dana arched a brow at him, and Kody turned red. "Of course, that's changed since I met you. I swear, once you mark me, I will be the most faithful wolf you ever saw. Why wouldn't I be when you make my wolf howl without even touching me?"

"Oh please." Dana laughed.

Kody's expression turned serious. "I mean it, Dana. Since I met you, I haven't even looked at another female, even the ones who've thrown themselves at me."

For a moment Dana saw green as the idea of women touching Kody—*my man*—roused a jealousy she'd never known she had in her.

Shaking off her possessive feelings, she turned with a smile to Nathan. "And I know you haven't been with anyone because you were looking and waiting for me."

Nathan shifted uncomfortably. "Um, that's not entirely true."

"What do you mean?" Dana asked.

"You left, and I wasn't sure if I would ever see you again. And"—his eyes dropped as he fiddled with his flatware—"well, a man's got needs."

She thought she misunderstood him. Surely, after all his claims of always loving her, he wouldn't have betrayed her with another woman? "Are you telling me you've slept with someone else?"

"You were gone, so yeah, I did. But they

meant nothing to me. I only ever loved you."

Dana heard a roaring in her head, and a sharp pain gripped her heart. "They? How many women have you fucked?" The crude word slipped out, and she saw Nathan wince.

"I don't know, a few. But not as many as Kody. Why the hell aren't you getting mad at him or John? It's not like they haven't buried their pricks in pussies other than yours." Nathan bristled, and Dana wanted to crawl into a hole and cry at her naïveté.

Tears filled her eyes. "But they're not the ones claiming they never stopped loving me or looking for me in the last twelve years."

"I was horny, and you were gone. What the fuck did you expect me to do?"

Dana understood with some part of her mind that she acted irrationally, not that she cared. The thought of Nathan touching another woman, pleasuring some slut like he'd pleasured her, drove her to it. And broke her heart. "You know, there's something called masturbation when you get horny and the one you love isn't around. Or, if your hands aren't good enough, then you should have invested in a fucking pocket pussy."

Nathan stood and glowered down at her. "Why the fuck would I do that when I could get the real thing anytime, anywhere?"

Dana stood and yelled back, even as tears spilled down her cheeks. "Because you said you loved me."

"I do love you, but you didn't expect me to stay celibate, did you? After all, you're the one who made it clear you wanted nothing to do with me and ran away."

"So why chase me then? Was it pride that made you come after me? 'Cause it certainly wasn't because your body couldn't live without me."

"I came after you because you're mine," he growled.

"You have a fine way of showing it," she retorted bitterly.

"Get off your fucking pedestal!" he shouted. "You were gone for twelve years. Are you trying to tell me that you spent the last twelve years by yourself and didn't let any other men touch you?"

"Pathetic, isn't it?" she cried. "The thought of letting another man touch me was repugnant. The one I wanted was you, and yet, apparently, you meant more to me than I did to you because you had no problem sticking your dick in another hole."

"It was just sex," he bellowed.

"Well, I hope it was worth it."

"You are such a fucking hypocrite. You talk about me like I'm some kind of man whore, and yet, I don't see you staying true to this love you supposedly have for me. Hell, only here two days and you're planning to mark and bed three of us."

She slapped him. "Make that two," she spat.

"Dana . . ." Nathan reached out for her, but Dana dodged his hands and ran for the stairs.

Tears blinded her as she took them by twos, but once at the top, she hesitated. She didn't want to go back to Nathan's room and the bed he'd probably fucked those sluts in. She followed her nose to another door and slipped in.

John's calming scent filled the space. She didn't pay attention to her surroundings. She crawled into the large bed that dominated the center of the room and hid under the covers.

Then she cried, her shoulders heaving as the rose-colored glasses she'd worn for the last twelve years shattered.

It seemed stupid, and naïve, of her to think Nathan hadn't moved on. And yet, she'd thought just that, especially when he'd come looking for her, declaring his love.

Why on earth did I think he'd never touched another woman? He was young, virile, and right about one thing—she'd left him. *But that never changed how I felt about him and what we shared.*

Dana had tried dating, but human males held no interest for her—a man she could snap in two just wasn't hot. Irrational as her jealousy was, she couldn't help the feelings of hurt.

She loved Nathan, but she had to admit there were parts of him that were a little domineering, and cocky. *But isn't that one of the things I love about him?* Ultimately that was what it boiled down to—she loved him, caveman mentality or not. However, she needed time to get over the shocking news that he hadn't stayed true.

She briefly thought of running, escaping the pain of yet another betrayal. But she'd grown out of the immature girl who'd escaped before when things got tough. Not to mention, she knew she could be happy here. Her fight with Nathan didn't change the fact that she still wanted what they offered.

However, one thing was sure; the order she'd claim the men had shuffled.

She wouldn't reward Nathan tonight, petty as it made her. He and his alpha attitude needed to realize she wouldn't bow or give in to him just because of his size or loud voice.

It's time he learned that he can't just order me around and treat my feelings like they're not important. If he loves me, then he's got to respect me.

And if it took punishing him by not marking him first to see he couldn't bully her around, then so be it.

It's not like claiming John will be a hardship. I can't wait to see my calm doctor lose control between my thighs.

Chapter Thirteen

Kody shook his head at Nathan. "You are such a fucking idiot sometimes."

Nathan glared at him. "What's that supposed to mean?"

"I think he means that bragging about how you fucked a ton of women and telling Dana she should accept it because it was her fault crossed a line," John replied.

Nathan scrubbed a hand through his hair. "What the hell else should I have done? Lied?"

John shook his head in disbelief. Nathan's male arrogance sometimes knew no bounds. "You could have tried playing it down instead of flaunting it. Couldn't you see how hurt she was to find out?"

"Dude, she is seriously upset," Kody added, peering with a frown in the direction of the stairs.

"What do you both care?" Nathan growled. "You heard what she said. She doesn't want me anymore." Nathan poured himself some more wine and took a swig of it.

"Give her time—" John started saying.

Nathan threw his wineglass at the wall,

where it shattered, spraying the red wine. "I'm tired of fucking waiting. I waited twelve goddamn years. What did she expect from me? Would you have stayed celibate for twelve years?"

Kody shrugged. "I've just met her, and I can say I don't understand how you could even look at another woman after having her. I haven't even thought of another female since she arrived in my life."

Nathan's gaze narrowed, and he tilted his head toward John. "And what do you have to say?"

John's jaw tightened, and he didn't give Nathan the excuse he was looking for to justify his actions.

"I would have never let her leave in the first place. Don't forget, I know the whole story. Despite your declarations of love, it took you five years before you seriously started looking for her and that only because the council passed on that report about the lone Lycan female who matched her description."

"I never forgot her," Nathan yelled.

"Then you did a piss-poor job of showing it," John shouted back. Like Kody, after having met Dana, feeling the connection between them, he couldn't imagine ever being with another woman, let alone dozens like Nathan had.

Nathan growled. "She left. I thought I'd

get over her like my dad and everyone kept saying. You think I didn't think of her when I fucked those other women? Do you think it wasn't her face I pictured? I know none of those women measured up to Dana. Maybe it was wrong of me to fuck everything with a pussy hole, but damn it, I wanted someone to take away the pain. But I learned my lesson, all right? I discovered I can't live without her. That there is no other woman who can satisfy both me and my beast. Why can't it be enough that I came to my senses finally and brought her back? Not that it does me any good. She doesn't want me."

"Maybe if you acted like a man in love instead of an alpha trying to dominate her at every turn, you wouldn't be in this position," John retorted. "You should have told her how much it hurt, how it took dating other women to realize she was the only one, instead of blaming her for the fact you were horny."

Nathan let out an inarticulate cry of rage, and muscles bunching in his shoulders, he grabbed the dinner table and upended it. The dishes cascaded off to crash and shatter on the floor. Nathan regarded the mess with glowering eyes. "You can both fuck right off. I don't need your advice. Besides, isn't this just perfect for you and Kody? I'm out of the picture now. You get her all to yourselves."

"That's not what either of us wanted,"

Kody said. "And I don't think it's what she wants either. Give her a chance to cool down, and you'll see. You just shocked her. Once she has a chance to think it over, she'll realize she can't be pissed at you for something you did while she was gone. Especially if you apologize and explain you did it 'cause you were lonely."

"I'll talk to her too," John replied, his anger at his friend warring with his pity for him and his pain. "Take the night to cool down and think of a way to make it up to her. Get her flowers or something. Make her breakfast in bed. Plan an apology speech."

Nathan's shoulders slumped. He turned to Kody. "What's your advice? You're the Casanova around here."

Kody grinned. "My plan is usually make her come until she forgets why she was mad in the first place. But somehow, I think trying that right now might go badly for you and your nuts. Come on. Have a beer with me while John-boy here goes and talks her down. I swear that man could talk a nun into dancing naked around a stripper pole if he tried."

Nathan's lips turned up into a smile at the attempted humor, but John could see the mirth never touched his eyes.

John left them nursing beers, Nathan sitting silent and dejected while Kody held up the one-sided conversation. John didn't like the simmer brewing under Nathan's seemingly calm surface. *Here's to hoping he sleeps his anger off and doesn't end up blowing his top like a volcano.*

John jogged up the stairs. He made to turn to the left in the direction of Nathan's room, where Dana had been sleeping, but a sniff of the air made him raise a brow in surprise. He followed her scent to the door of his room. He paused outside, listening to the stifled sobs from inside, barely noticeable over the murmur of voices from downstairs. John hesitated before entering because logic said Nathan wouldn't like that Dana had searched for comfort in John's room.

He'll like it even less if I go in there and something happens between us. But while John wanted to aspire to an altruistic nature, selfish desire, and a burgeoning love for the woman inside, made him not care what Nathan thought. *He had his chance and fucked it up.*

John intended to make things right again between Dana and Nathan, but at the same time, he was only a man. *A man who will do anything to make her happy. Anything . . .*

* * * *

Dana cried into the pillow, her tears soaking the fabric. How could she not when she heard Nathan bellowing? A part of her ached to go to him, to clasp him in her arms and say all was forgiven.

Another part of her feared that, by caving to him, he'd think nothing of hurting her again in the future. She covered her ears with her hands, unwilling to listen to his obvious anger and distress. A light touch on her shoulder made her thrash wildly, her flailing fists striking flesh.

She rolled and opened her burning eyes, expecting to see Nathan, come to hunt her down and beg her forgiveness—or force it. Instead, she found herself wrapped in John's arms, his soothing presence a balm to her turmoil. Her tears flowed anew. He dragged her onto his lap as she sobbed, stroking her hair and rocking her as she wept for the twelve years of her life that she'd wasted running. Wept for the life she could have had if she'd only looked past her fears. Wept because she couldn't stem the pain that, once again, she'd experienced, even if unthinking, at Nathan's hands.

"I am such an idiot," she finally sniffled. "I mean why wouldn't he have found someone else?"

"I'd like to be a dick right now and say he shouldn't have, but truthfully, I can't blame him. And hate me for my words if you want, but he did the right thing. The only thing he could do in his situation. He didn't know if he'd ever see you again. I know firsthand how lonely and lost he was after you were gone."

Dana hiccupped. "I kn-know. But it

hurts. All those years I spent alone, I figured he did too."

John brushed the tears from her cheeks. "Just because he wasn't alone didn't mean he was happy. Nathan wasn't lying when he said he loved you all that time. But it took bedding those women to realize none of them could replace you."

Dana sniffled. "A rational part of me understands that, but the selfish part is pissed and hurt."

"Then hit me. Take out some of your frustration."

Dana craned her head back to peer at his face. He returned her gaze with a calm brown-eyed one. "Are you insane? Why would I do that?"

John grinned. "Because sometimes hitting things feels good."

Dana gave him a weak chuckle. "Thanks for the offer, but I couldn't hurt you." Seated on his lap, her tears at bay, she noticed how nice his arms felt wrapped around her. She inhaled his scent, and her wolf stirred, along with a primal hunger. Awareness of him as a man flooded her senses, bringing a tingling arousal with it. "Actually," she murmured, "I can think of a better way of relieving my frustration." She reached up to cup his face in her hands and kissed him.

Earlier she'd thought about doing this as

part of a revenge against Nathan, but encased in John's arms, she could admit that she was just using that as an excuse to touch him. She wanted John, wanted him in her life and as one of her mates. With him, there was none of the chaos she got with Nathan, none of the naughty playfulness that she saw with Kody. John was like a rock—steady, dependable, and hard where she needed him.

He broke the embrace, his breathing ragged and his erection firm against her bottom. "I don't want to be used as a way of getting back at Nathan," he warned.

Dana stroked his cheeks and smiled at him. "Oh, don't worry. I have many uses for you, and I'm afraid they all have to do with pleasuring me. This is probably going to sound corny, but I think I'm falling in love with you."

Apparently that was all the answer he needed. His arms crushed her tight to him as his lips found hers in a torrid kiss that stole her breath.

They fell back on the bed, his heavier weight atop her body. She loved it and could have kissed him all night, but her body clamored for more. John, as if sensing this, slid his lips away from her mouth down to the column of her throat. He kissed her pulse, and her breathing hitched. He shifted his body to the side, and she opened her eyes.

"Are you sure?" he asked. "Once we

start, I don't know if I'll have the willpower to stop."

"Make me yours, John." She grasped the edge of the dress she'd worn to dinner and pulled it up.

With her head caught in the fabric, he took advantage and rubbed his face on the soft skin of her belly. She untangled herself and saw him staring with smoldering eyes at her underwear.

"Please tell me that isn't a thong," he said, his voice husky. She rolled over, and he groaned. "Damn. I am so glad I didn't know that at dinner, or I would never have managed to eat—well, food anyway," he ended with a tease.

His breath brushed the skin of her buttocks as he placed a kiss on each cheek. Dana trembled, and the thin fabric, stretched taut across her cleft, moistened.

"You smell so good," he murmured, his face pressing against the crease of her thighs where they met her ass.

She parted her legs, and he fanned his warm breath over her sex. The wet tip of his tongue traced the material that barely covered her mound, an erotic touch that brought forth a moan. The sound emboldened him, or so it seemed, because he grasped the string with his teeth and, with a growl, snapped it. Dana held her breath as she waited for his next move, a long, wet lick across the length of her slit.

"Oh." Again, he laved her, probing between her lips, thrusting his tongue into her pussy. Dana clutched at the sheets on his bed, her body afire.

He pulled back, his breathing ragged. "Roll over," he demanded, softened with a, "please."

She did as he asked. His head returned to its spot between her thighs, and he licked her before circling his tongue around her clit. He used his lips to hold and suck on her sensitive flesh, and she bucked involuntarily. He placed his hands on her stomach and held her down, pinned her as he tortured her clit with his mouth. She moaned, and her head arched back as he drew her desire taut. Then stopped.

She opened her eyes, prepared to beg him to continue, and was caught by his burning gaze, and the fact that he still wore clothes.

She went to her knees and tugged at his shirt. He stripped it off, exposing his lean, hard body. She stroked her hand down his lightly furred chest until she reached the barrier of his pants. He aided her in unsnapping them. Then he left the bed to stand for a moment to pull them off. Clothing shed, she could clearly see his erect cock, which curved slightly at the end and jutted proudly from his loins.

John returned to kneel on the bed before her. She reached out a hand and ran it down his

Eve Langlais

hard belly to his rod, but he caught her hand before she could grasp him.

"Save that for later. I don't think I can handle that right now."

Dana smiled at him, pleased at his lack of control. The calm doctor kneeling in front of her already looked wild, and they'd only just begun. "So does that mean I'm not allowed to give you my first-ever BJ?" Something she'd read about but never actually experienced. A fact she'd rectify very soon.

He growled at her and clasped her body to his, the skin-to-skin contact scorching. More moist heat pooled in her cleft, and she moaned at the feel of his hard cock pressing against her belly. His lips latched onto hers, and she opened her mouth to him, allowing their tongues to clash in a wet duel.

Her nipples pebbled against his chest, and as if sensing their presence, their burgeoning desire, John leaned her back so that he could bend and take one into his mouth.

Dana moaned as his tongue swirled around the tip. Her pelvis bucked forward, trying to get closer to him.

John growled, and she opened eyelids heavy with desire to see his eyes glowing, his expression intent—and fucking gorgeous.

"God, Dana. I wanted to take things slow, but you're making me lose control."

"Good. I don't want to wait any longer.

Make love to me, John." She didn't think she'd survive if he didn't sink into her and do something about the fire that raged in her body. Her wolf was also an impatient presence in her mind, pacing and whining, the urge to bite him, mark him, growing stronger by the second.

He drew her forward for a kiss, a deep and passionate one that she returned just as fiercely. His hands clasped her about the waist, and he pulled her forward until she straddled his lap, his cock sitting hotly under her cleft.

She rubbed herself against his length, covering him in her cream. He caught her hint. The head of his prick probed the entrance to her sex. Natural instinct guided her. She tilted her hips to ease his angle of entry. He slid in slowly, drawing out the pleasure, but Dana was impatient. She thrust down onto him, seating him fully inside.

She threw her head back and let out a gasp at the sensation. He filled her snugly, his cock buried to the hilt and butting deliciously up inside her. His fingers dug into her hips as her pussy squeezed around him, sending a quivering sensation through her.

"Oh," she exclaimed at the bliss that shot through her. She rocked against him, and again her channel quivered.

"Jesus, Dana," he groaned. With his hands gripping her tight, he bounced her on his cock, sheathing and retreating his hard length in a way that made Dana's breathing come faster and faster. Her nails dug into his shoulders as the pleasure coiled inside her.

A scream built in her throat as he held her on the edge of glory. She opened her eyes and beheld perfection. The cords in John's neck stood out, and his eyes blazed with passion as he claimed her body carnally. But she wanted more than just sex from him. *I want him, body, wolf, and soul.* She leaned forward and kissed the taut skin of his pecs, just above his heart. His heart beat in a mad cadence that resonated inside her. She opened her mouth wide on the wet spot she'd created, and her wolf bounded forward eagerly in her mind. Her incisors lengthened, and she bit him.

John roared and bucked, his hips bolting straight up as his hands on her hips pushed down. Dana didn't let go of him until she'd tasted and swallowed a mouthful of his coppery blood. In the distance, she heard howling, but she blocked her mind to it. Tonight was for the man who'd given her what she needed.

She'd no sooner loosened her latch than he laid her back in one fluid motion so that he rested between her thighs, his body thrusting into her furiously.

"Mine," he growled. Then he reciprocated and sank his own teeth into the soft flesh of her breast.

Dana screamed as the bond between

them came full circle. Blood to blood. Soul to soul. The euphoria of it triggered an orgasm so intense that she screamed again, bucking wildly under John, who, with a bellow of his own, shot his seed deep inside her.

They clung to each other tightly with ragged breaths as the bliss wrung them dry. When their heart rates began to slow and their bodies relaxed from their blissful tension, John kissed her gently.

"I love you, Dana. From this day forth and forever more, no matter our paths, no matter our destiny, I am by your side. You no longer walk alone."

Dana opened eyes brimming with tears. The beauty of his words and, even more astonishing, the sincerity stole her voice. She hugged him to her tightly and hoped he understood how much she appreciated his gift.

Then in case he didn't understand the mental vibes she threw his way, she showed him in a carnal way that left no doubt as to what she thought.

Chapter Fourteen

Dana slept spooned with John—*my mate*—after making love a second time. Held in his protective embrace, the hum of their bond almost visible, she discovered inner peace. Even better, she'd lost her anger and hurt over Nathan's actions of the past. After talking with John, she could more clearly understand why Nathan had done it, and she regretted her jealous reaction of the previous day.

Now here's to hoping he's not too pissed about me marking John first. Even if he was, she'd practice patience. They'd both hurt each other, and the time had arrived for it to stop. She loved Nathan, and he loved her. The past needed to be pushed aside in favor of the future, a bright future with her back in the heart of a pack and surrounded by love—both the mental and physical kind.

Lost in her thoughts, she didn't realize John had woken until a firm poke against her backside announced his ready state. She wiggled against it.

"Minx," he growled in her ear, tugging the lobe with his teeth.

"Admit it, you love it."

John chuckled. "Yes, I do, and I love you. But much as I'd like to pleasure my new mate this morning, I think that might be pushing it a bit far, given the unresolved situation waiting for us."

Dana sighed. "He's going to be hurt. I know."

"What are you planning to do?"

"Talk to him first and apologize for freaking out. Then, if we can put our differences behind us, I was thinking of marking him next. Are you all right with that?" she asked, craning to peer back at John.

His gentle brown eyes met hers. "I'm not jealous or afraid if that's what you're asking. Mark Nathan and Kody when you feel the time is right. I won't put up a fuss. I was always taught to share well with others."

Dana gasped at his comment and jabbed him with an elbow. "Now you sound like Kody," she chided.

John chuckled. "No, Kody would have said I can't wait until I share you with the others—naked."

"Mmm. Sounds like a plan," she purred.

"W-what?" John stuttered. "Are you screwing with me?"

"Not yet, but I plan to later, and maybe we won't be alone."

Dana wiggled out of his grasp and dashed

to the bathroom, laughter bubbling forth at John's pained, "Dana!"

When she returned after peeing and brushing her teeth, she found him, unfortunately, dressed.

His eyes glowed as he took in her naked body, and he hugged her to him. She clung to him, wishing they could stay hidden for a while longer, basking in their bond. But she refused to take the easy way out.

"I guess it's time to face the music," she said, nervous at the prospect of facing the others, most especially Nathan.

"You know what? Let me go scope the situation with Nathan out first and make sure he has removed his foot from his mouth."

Dana knew it was cowardly of her to let John den the possibly rabid wolf, but she didn't want to shatter the fragile happiness she'd found. *I've got a mate now to help me shoulder things. I no longer have to face everything alone.*

"Everything will work out," John said before kissing her softly and leaving.

I wish I shared his optimism. Dana wouldn't hold her breath, though. What she'd done, fantastic as it had been, would hurt Nathan. And while she loved him, and intended to mark him in due course, what had happened couldn't be changed, nor did she regret it.

Dana had no toiletries or clothing in John's room, but that didn't mean she couldn't face the day clean. She returned to the bathroom. She turned the shower on hot and stepped under its soothing spray. Given her frantic lovemaking with John the previous night, she'd expected to be sore, but instead energy imbued her and made her smile. She even sang as she bathed.

Her skin scrubbed pink and clean, she stepped from the steamy cubicle and grabbed a towel. She wiped her body down and then wrapped it around herself before stepping back out into the bedroom. And stopped dead.

Nathan lounged on John's bed, his hands laced under his head. She could smell the stench of alcohol from where she stood. She also couldn't miss the menacing glow in his eyes. Nathan's wolf sat very close to the surface, and with the alcohol lowering the barrier between man and beast, she should tread carefully.

"Morning, Nathan," she said cautiously.

"Maybe for you," he replied with a glare. "Tell me, was he a good fuck?" Nathan's words slurred together, and a shiver of trepidation went down her spine.

"I'm not answering that."

"Why not?" he taunted. "I mean it can't be because you're afraid of hurting my feelings."

"You're drunk."

"Gee, I wonder why. Could it be because the woman I loved was fucking and marking another man?"

Dana winced. Said so baldly, she sounded like a vile bitch. But she refused to let him beat her down with words and to dirty something so beautiful. "It wasn't like that."

Nathan jumped up off the bed and strode to her, bristling with tension. "Oh, how was it then?" He encroached upon her space, his looming form sending a shiver through her. "I know you enjoyed it. I heard you," he snarled through gritted teeth. "I felt it when you marked him. Were you laughing at me when you did it?"

Tears rolled down her cheeks as his pain washed over her. "Nathan, don't do this. I still love you. I want to make you one of my mates."

"So why didn't you mark me first then? You were supposed to be mine," he roared.

She realized there would be no getting through to him while the alcohol held him prisoner. "I think you need to calm down," she said, backing away from him.

"No, I'm done waiting for you to make up your goddamn mind. I just want what you gave him. Fuck this taking my time shit and giving you space." His eyes glowered fiercely, and she saw the tip of his incisors, which had dropped in his mouth.

Oh shit. Dana whirled to run, but Nathan caught her, his iron grip inescapable.

He lifted her and brought her up to eye level, and tears brimmed in her eyes. "Please, Nathan, don't do it. Not like this. Please."

"You forced me to it. You're mine, Dana. I might have to share you, but damn it, you will belong to me."

She pummeled his chest as he drew her in close, but there was no stopping him. He didn't soften his action. He didn't even attempt to seduce her. He just bit her—hard. Pain shot through her without the endorphins to soften it.

Dana screamed shrilly. Nathan loosened one hand to muffle her cry, and she bit him, unthinkingly. At the metallic taste of his blood in her mouth, lightning struck without the beauty of the night before and completed the circle of shared blood.

A moment later, she found herself torn from Nathan's grasp, and she sobbed against Kody's chest, the pain in her shoulder throbbing as it oozed.

"What the fuck?" she heard John yell.

"She's mine," growled Nathan.

"And she was intending to mark you when you stopped acting like a fucking Neanderthal."

"So what's the big fucking deal? I just did what she intended to do," Nathan replied in a thick voice, his belligerent tone not the least contrite. "Now, why don't you and the puppy leave so I can fuck my new mate?"

Dana heard the sound of flesh striking flesh. She turned in Kody's arms to see John methodically beating Nathan, who, drunk off his ass, responded too slowly to defend himself.

"Stop," she whispered then louder, "Stop!"

John delivered one last blow that made Nathan drop to his knees and keel over. John glared down at his unconscious alpha before he strode over to her.

Kody handed her over and shook his head. "I can't fucking believe he did that. I knew he was upset, but I never expected him to attack her like that."

"He lost control, and he'll be lucky if the council doesn't execute him for it."

Dana blanched. Unclaimed females could be mated by force under archaic laws, but Dana wasn't unmated, not since the previous night. What Nathan had done was tantamount to rape, the esoteric kind. "You can't tell."

John's brows shot up. "Are you kidding me? He forced you to mate with him."

"He only did what I should have done in the first place. If there's any fault, it's mine for not marking him first. I knew how much it meant to him."

John gritted his teeth. "Fine."

Dana rested her head against John's shoulders and shook. *This is all my fault.*

"What do I do with him?" Kody asked.

"I don't give a fuck," John growled.

"Put him to bed." Dana knew she should hate Nathan for what he'd done, but instead, guilt ate her as she took responsibility for his actions. She'd pushed him to this by not choosing him first, by allowing her own hurt over the past to cloud her judgment.

Dana let John lead her to the bed to sit down as Kody hefted Nathan, with some difficulty, in a fireman hold and staggered out with him.

"I'm sorry, Dana," John apologized. "I went looking for him and couldn't find him. Kody said he'd last seen him going for a run in the woods. I never expected he'd do this."

"If it's anyone's fault, it's mine. I should have marked him first." At the sight of John's lips tightening, she hastened to say, "I don't regret what happened last night. I loved every minute of it, and I'm glad you're one of my mates. But"—she sighed, and her shoulders slouched, causing her weeping wound to ache— "I should have done things differently."

"Different how?" John asked as he stood. He went over to his closet and pulled out a bag. He rummaged around and pulled some antiseptic from his bag and proceeded to wipe the gouges in her shoulder.

"Well, maybe if I'd taken you all at the same time, no one would have felt left out." At John's shocked looked, she smiled. "Shut up. I know I am the last person you expected to hear that from, but honestly, short of a tag-team session, I don't see how anyone wouldn't have gotten hurt."

"So does this mean you're going to mark Kody sooner than later?" John asked carefully.

"Talking about me?"

Dana's head shot up as Kody strolled back into the room. She still sat there in the buff, her towel lost in the action, but she didn't have the energy for embarrassment. "Yes, I want to mark you if you still want me after all the crap that's happened."

"Take your time," Kody replied, dropping to a knee before her, his green eyes looking up at hers with a serious intensity. "Unlike my alpha, I can handle waiting for my turn, and I'm good at sharing."

Dana leaned forward and kissed Kody lightly. "I can't wait to experience that. But for now, I think I need some clothes and food."

However, she couldn't stop the stir of excitement Kody's words had engendered. If one wolf loving her was explosive, how would two feel? Or, even more decadent, if things ever got resolved with Nathan, three?

* * * *

Nathan groaned as he rolled in his bed, his head throbbing painfully from a hangover to end all hangovers, but even more strange, his jaw and face ached as well. *What the fuck happened?*

Fragments came back to him: the fight with Dana—another fuck-up in his courtship of her. He'd owe her an apology for acting like such an ass, something he should have done the night before instead of sending John straight into her arms while he turned to drinking beer. Lots of it. He recalled deciding to get sloshed once he realized John and Dana were making love and then mated.

A pang of hurt, tinged with some jealousy, hit him. He'd truly wanted to be first, but instead, he'd allowed his stubborn nature to send another man to her when she was vulnerable.

The rest of the evening was a blur as he'd drowned his pain in alcohol.

But it didn't explain his sore face. He rolled out of his bed, a bed he didn't remember staggering to, and stumbled over to a mirror. He let out a low whistle at what he saw. Bruises covered his visage, as if he'd taken a beating.

More hazy memories bombarded him, including one of Dana regarding him with fear and pleading. Realization hit him like a ton of bricks, and he sank to his knees, moaning.

"No. Oh no. What have I done?" he whispered, clutching his head.

"I see you've remembered."

Lost in his misery, Nathan hadn't noticed John entering, but he didn't miss the cold anger in his tone. "Please tell me it's a nightmare. Tell me I didn't force my mark on her," Nathan pleaded.

"I'm not into lying."

Nathan swayed in horror. He pounded the floor, anger rising in him—at himself. "How could I do that to her?"

"You tell me," John said. "I understand you wanted to be first, but if there's one thing Dana told you over and over, it was that she wanted to choose the when and where."

"And she chose you," Nathan replied. His previous jealousy over that fact vanished in the face of his greater travesty.

"But she wanted it to be you. I want you to know I went to her and pled your case. She made the choice to mark me first. I'm sorry I didn't have the strength or will to turn her down. I hope you'll accept my apology and responsibility for what happened."

Nathan's head shot up—a little quickly—and his stomach lurched. "Don't you fucking dare. I'm not some coward to hide from my actions. Had I not let my own pride and determination blind me, I would have gone up to talk to her instead of you. If I had, then things might well have been different. Instead, I chose to wallow in self-pity and alcohol. I lost control, and no matter the reason, there is no excuse. I'll pack my things and be gone within the hour."

John inhaled sharply. "What the fuck are

you talking about? Who said anything about you leaving?"

"I can't stay here. Seeing her, seeing her fear of me. Knowing I can never have her."

"God, you are such an idiot," John exclaimed, his exasperation clear. "Yes, she was scared when you forced the mark on her, but who do you think stopped me from killing you? Dana doesn't want you to go. She still loves you and blames herself for what happened."

Nathan snorted. He didn't believe that.

"He's telling the truth."

Nathan whipped his head around at the soft sound of Dana's voice. A wave of dizziness caught up to him, and he almost fell over. "Dana . . ." he whispered.

"It's all right, Nathan. I shouldn't have hurt you like I did."

Nathan closed his eyes at the recrimination in her eyes, not directed at him but herself. "No, not you too. I did this. Me and my jealousy and my temper."

The light tread of her steps approached as John's heavy ones receded. The door clicked shut a moment before she clasped his bowed head to her body.

"Don't beat yourself up over it. It's happened. It's over with. Let's just move on."

Nathan, for the first time since Dana had left him twelve years ago, felt tears moisten his eyes. *She might be able to forgive me, but how do I forgive myself?*

She tilted his head and forced him to look at her. He wanted to see hate in her expression, disdain for him, anything but the love that shone in her eyes. A love he didn't deserve.

I need to get her to leave me alone before I fuck things up even worse. He also needed to leave the compound so that she could get a chance at the happiness she'd earned.

"I want to start afresh. Make things right." She smiled at him and brushed her lips over his.

Nathan shuddered, pushing down the need to let himself take what she offered. "Listen, I'm still pretty wrung out from all the drinking and stuff. Not to mention, I reek. Why don't you get Kody and John to take you to the movies while I catch a few more hours' sleep? I'll make dinner for when you guys get back."

Her brow knitted in a frown as she stared at him. "Why do I get the feeling you're hiding something from me?"

"I'm really tired," he lied.

"Let me help you to bed then." She tugged him up from the floor and walked him to his bed. He climbed in and let her tuck him in. Her hand smoothed his hair from his brow, and she leaned down to brush his lips.

"I love you, Nathan."

"I love you, too," he answered through a

voice gone thick. He closed his eyes before she saw the dreaded tears.

She left, and Nathan lay there waiting. He dozed off for a while but woke when he heard the sounds of them leaving.

He wasted no time. He sprang out of bed. Regardless of what she and John said, he'd lost his right to stay.

His cell phone rang as he readied himself. *What does the Lycan council want now?* He answered, and his brows drew together at their message.

It looked as if he had one more task to do before he left Dana to live a life of happiness. Something to keep her safe.

Chapter Fifteen

Sitting in a dark movie theater with a mate on one side and a man she planned to mate with on the other proved interesting. Make that titillating.

Dana held the popcorn bucket on her lap, and every time they dug into the buttery box, she couldn't help wishing their hands were diving for a different snack. The darkness thankfully hid her blushes, but it couldn't stop her arousal.

John draped an arm over her shoulder and bent to whisper, "Are you okay?"

She turned toward him and leaned in close, but instead of speaking, she kissed him. His body went rigid for a moment before he kissed her back.

When she moaned against his mouth, frustrated that he wasn't stripping her for more, he pulled back, his breathing ragged. "Behave. We're in public."

Dana made a face at him and slumped in her seat. A hand brushed her thigh from the other side, and she peered sideways to see Kody watching the screen as his hand flattened itself on her thigh then began sliding her skirt up.

She bit her lip but didn't stop him, not with her core pulsing, aching for his touch. John leaned over her and removed the creeping hand. She made a frustrated sound. A part of her mind watched, appalled that she acted so wanton, but it didn't stop the urges. Her usual control was being tested, not only by her body's newfound needs but by her wolf, which clamored to mark the other she'd chosen. *To claim my final mate.*

She thrust her hand out and laid it on Kody's thigh. Her fingers hadn't crept far when she heard John sigh. "Come on. Time to go."

"Yes, Father," Kody replied as he covered her hand with his.

Dana giggled. She stood and followed John out of the dark movie theater, Kody right behind her.

When she stumbled, his hands caught her around the waist and pulled her back into him, close enough for her to notice how happy her closeness made him. She rubbed back against him, and Kody gripped her tighter.

John turned around. "Would you two stop screwing around?" he hissed, but she could hear the mirth in his tone. "Wait until we get out of the theater at least."

Dana blushed at her she-wolf-in-heat behavior and, even worse, in front of John, the man she'd so recently taken to mate. But she couldn't help herself. Her hormones raged out of control. Her wolf didn't help matters with her pacing and yipping demands that she mark the blond one.

Kody curved his arm around her waist and swept her along to catch up to John, who hugged her other side. They made it outside and walked to the SUV.

Before John swung into the driver's seat, he tugged Dana to him and lowered his head to capture her lips in a searing kiss. Dana's knees buckled. "Get in the backseat with Kody," he murmured.

"Why? I rode into town in the front seat."

John kissed her again, his hands squeezing her buttocks. "Once we hit the woods, I'll pull over so you can claim him."

"But—"

"Dana, we can all feel it, the pull inside you, the need of your wolf to claim him. Let's get it done before we get back to the house."

"What about you?"

John gave her a crooked smile. "I'll be watching to make sure the pup does it right."

Instant moisture flooded her cleft, and she didn't protest any further as they bundled her into the backseat. She expected to be embarrassed at the way they both assumed she wanted to make out with Kody in the backseat like a schoolgirl. Apparently they knew her better than she knew herself.

She ended up in his lap at the first touch of his lips on hers, the hard bulge of his cock under her bottom exciting her. Kody's hands roved over her body as he kissed her, his tongue sliding sinuously between her lips to taste her. He drew her tongue into his mouth and sucked it, an erotic gesture that sent an electric bolt straight to her pussy. The scent of her arousal filled the vehicle.

Kody left her lips and leaned her back to duck his head so he could tug at a nipple protruding through the fabric of her dress. Her head lolled back, and she caught a glimpse of John in the rearview mirror. His eyes glowed, and his lips curved into a sexy smile. Whatever thought she'd had about it being weird to be watched vanished in that moment. Having an audience excited her, and while she didn't know how to voice it aloud, her pussy creamed in response. *If this is how I feel with John spying on me making out, then how would it feel if he decided to join in?*

Kody distracted her with his hand sliding under her bunched-up skirt to press against her wet cleft.

"Find a spot," Kody growled, confusing Dana until she realized he meant John, who veered the SUV off the road, heading into the trees for cover.

The passenger door opened, and John

pulled her out. Dana regarded him with passion-glazed eyes.

She squeaked in surprise when Kody pressed in from behind, grinding his groin into her backside and pushing her into John. Pinned between them, Dana almost swooned.

"She's wearing too much clothes," Kody growled.

"Then we should fix that problem." John took a step back and grabbed the hem of her dress. He lifted it off her in one fluid motion. Dana shivered more from what was to come than the cold.

John stripped off his shirt and tossed it to the side and unbuttoned his pants, letting his cock spring forth. When she reached out to touch him, he shook his head and stepped back. He gripped his cock and stroked it. "Kody first."

Kody pressed up against her from behind, his clothes shed while she'd watched John strip. His cock, thick and hard, pressed against her, and she trembled.

"Bend over," he ordered gruffly. "Show me that beautiful pussy of yours."

Oh God. His dirty words sent cream rushing to her cleft, but she did as asked and bent over. He ran a hand down the crevice of her ass, pulling the string of her thong aside to dip a finger into her sex.

Dana moaned. Hearing movement, she

opened her eyes and saw John's cock bob into view. He fisted it as he watched Kody fondle her from behind.

"She tastes like honey," he advised.

"Mmm, and I love honey," Kody drawled before placing his hot mouth on her.

Dana's knees buckled, but hands—more than one set—caught her and held her up. Those hands roved across her body, dipping under to toy with her pebbled nipples. Kody flicked his tongue against her clit, making her gasp and shudder, the pleasure driving her wild.

He inserted one finger then two into her wet channel, pumping her with his digits. Dana couldn't help herself. She came, her body shuddering at all the sensations.

But they weren't done.

A cock probed her entrance, a big cock. Kody eased himself into her, his girth stretching her and triggering aftershocks that caused him to grunt.

"Damn she's tight." His naughty compliment made her sex clench further, and his fingers dug into her ass cheeks.

"Fuck her," John whispered. "Give it to her hard."

Dana keened, the knowledge that John watched Kody as he penetrated her a forbidden excitement that made the moment all the more erotic.

Kody pumped her, slowly, each thrust

into her butting up against a sensitive spot inside that made her gasp and squeeze.

"I want to see her sucking your cock," Kody grunted as he kept slapping into her flesh.

Dana opened her eyes as something came in contact with her mouth. John held his cock positioned in front of her. She'd never sucked a rod before, but she was game to try. She opened her mouth, and John slid it in.

At first, she wasn't sure what to do. John thankfully pumped his shaft in and out of her mouth as she experimented running her tongue around it, something that made John hiss, "Yes, that's it. Now suck on it."

Dana did as told and suctioned him, finding a rhythm in his oral thrusts and an enjoyment in pleasuring him.

Kody thrust into her faster, his body slapping up against her ass. John matched his pace, and Dana just about lost her mind. An orgasm hovered just out of reach, and yet, while she sat close, she didn't crest. Every time she'd come close to peaking, Kody would slow down and even withdraw his cock. It drove her nuts.

She sucked at John's cock more frantically, trying to imbue her urgency, and John's fingers threaded in her hair.

"That's it, sweetheart. Fuck me, I'm gonna come." John thrust himself deep into her mouth, and suddenly Dana had to swallow as a salty liquid filled her mouth. She kept pulling and sucking at John's prick until, with a laugh, he pulled his cock free with a wet sound.

"Enough, you little minx. Hey, bro, let's try that move we talked about."

What? They discussed moves?

Callused hands bent her back upright, but Kody's cock remained buried in her. She wondered how this would work as the new angle didn't exactly give him the deep penetration she longed for.

John dropped to one knee and lifted her legs to pull them over his shoulders, putting his mouth straight in line with her clit.

Oh my fucking God. Dana screamed as they showed her just how well this new position worked. Kody clamped an arm around her waist and began bouncing her on his very thick cock as John flicked his tongue on her clit. Faster and faster they both moved, the full sensation in her pussy along with the intense pleasure on her clit bringing her to the edge of bliss and crossing it. Her orgasm hit her with the weight of a freight train, sending her body into convulsions, the fabulous, never-ending kind.

Caught up in her intense pleasure, she barely noticed it when Kody leaned forward and sank in his teeth into her shoulder as his hot juice jetted into her and marked her womb.

The frantic pumping slowed, and Dana retained enough of her wits to realize she had yet to mark Kody. Her body still quivered with aftershocks. Dana turned into Kody's arms and looked up into his bright eyes.

With a smile, she growled, "Mine." Then she sank her sharp incisors into his flesh as her wolf howled joyously in her mind.

The blood of her third mate hit her tongue, and she swallowed his coppery essence, closing the circle and binding him to her irrevocably. When she opened her eyes again and looked up at him, he gazed down at her with wonder in his eyes.

"I love you, Dana," he whispered. "I will forever worship you and strive to make you the happiest woman alive."

She hugged him tight as she kissed him. John pressed in against her back, and she leaned her head back to give him a kiss as well. She was now mated to three men, and she couldn't be happier.

The future is looking bright, and what do you know? Two was better than one. Now, to make things up with Nathan because now I've got to know how it works with three.

Chapter Sixteen

Dana giggled quite a bit as they hunted for their clothes and brushed them off. Her cheeks heated a few times at her mates' ribald remarks, but surprisingly, even now that the ardor had worn off, she didn't regret a thing.

In the space of less than a week, she'd gone from hiding from a mating situation to becoming part of a polyamorous group with three men. *Ain't love grand?*

They crowded back into the SUV with Dana sitting on Kody's lap in the front seat and John holding her hand and driving with his free one. A need to remain close to them imbued her, especially as the sky darkened and they approached the compound.

Once again, she feared Nathan's reaction, especially once he realized she'd marked Kody. *I've got to stop letting my hormones make my decisions* because, in truth, making things right with Nathan should have come before her frolic and claiming of Kody. But nestled in his arms, his lips brushing the top of her head, she couldn't muster the strength to regret her choice.

They're all mine now, and the sooner Nathan

comes to grips with it, the happier we'll all be. Besides, with John's impromptu lesson, I now can suck cock. If that doesn't make Nathan forgive me, then I don't know what will.

They were buzzed into the compound by the pair of wolves on guard at the gate, and Dana became more tense the closer they came to home.

Kody squeezed her. "Don't worry. We won't let anything happen to you."

Dana didn't worry for herself. *Who will protect Nathan from himself?*

They pulled into the gravel drive, and a chill invaded her at the sight of the dark house. "Why are the lights off?" she whispered.

John frowned as he turned off the ignition. "Maybe he was more tired than he thought and is still sleeping."

Dana wanted to believe him, but a sense of foreboding grew. Kody and John, as if sensing her dread, stuck close to her as they walked in. The house was shrouded in silence. Kody flicked on a switch and flooded the place with light.

"I'll go check upstairs," John announced.

"Maybe he's outside getting wood," Kody said, his own tone implying he didn't believe it.

Dana wandered into the cold kitchen and knew Nathan was gone. Her stomach plummeted when she saw the white envelope with her name slashed in blue ink across it sitting on the counter. She grabbed it and smelled Nathan on the parchment.

She opened it with trembling hands, her vision blurring after the first sentence. Sobbing, she collapsed to the floor, her heart breaking.

Footsteps came running, and as Kody pulled her up into the shelter of his arms, John tugged the letter from her hands and read it aloud.

Dana,

I can never express how sorry I am for losing control like I did, but even worse, was your understanding. There is no excuse for my behavior. Jealousy has no place in a pack and even less place in a mated group. By my actions, I've proven myself unworthy. You deserve so much better. At least you'll find that with John and Kody. I felt through the bond that you marked Kody, and I wanted to say I'm glad. I don't want you to ever be alone again or to live a life on the run.

I know you don't have it in your heart to make me leave like I should for my actions. So, I'm going to leave of my own volition knowing it's for the best, and in time, you will realize it too. As a parting gift and apology for my actions, I've gone to challenge the rogue who held you captive. It won't erase what I've done to you, but I can at least give you peace of mind and a home you can live in without fear. I love you, Dana. Be happy.

Always yours, Nathan

"Stupid fucking idiot," she cursed through her tears. "We have to go after him."

"Of course we will," Kody murmured, stroking her back as he held her shuddering body.

"We'll go after him," John corrected. "You will stay here where it's safe."

"No. This is my fault. I have to go. I have to make him see reason."

John sighed. "I guess, short of handcuffing you to a bed, you aren't going to listen, are you?"

Dana smiled at him tremulously. "If you ever want sex again, you'll let me come with you."

Kody gasped in mock horror. "Darling, that's just cruel."

"Fine. You can come with us, but you stay behind and keep out of trouble. We'll do the fighting, and once we're done, you get the job of telling Nathan's he's an idiot."

And then once I'm done yelling at him for scaring me to death, I am going to strip him naked and prove how much he means to me.

* * * *

Nathan dropped his duffel bag by the large oak in the clearing where, a lifetime ago, he'd made love to Dana. It seemed only fitting to him that he make his stand in the place where his life had changed and shaped him into the man who now needed to escape. The irony of the situation didn't escape him. *She ran because she didn't want to be shared, and now it's my turn to run because my jealousy couldn't handle it.*

But he wouldn't leave until he could assure himself of her safety, and that meant clearing out the rogues. A part of him screamed at himself for stupidly coming to face them alone. How many times had he drummed into his pack the need to not leave the compound at night unless they were in large groups? What made him think he alone could handle the menace? Sure, he possessed more strength than his brothers of the fur, and he had the unique ability to half shift into a beast—an ability that only the ones with the most control could achieve--but still, he was only one wolf against who knew how many. Not exactly great odds. Of course, at this point, he also didn't care if he lived or died.

How does that Bon Jovi song go that Dana loved so much? Going down in a blaze of glory or something?

He stripped his shirt off and laid it on his bag. He flexed his muscles as he kicked off his shoes. His track pants he left on for now. Menacing threats and intimidation were never as effective among men when naked with their pricks swinging about.

Unless you're hung like Kody.

Nathan's mind skittered as it avoided the coming confrontation that might very well see him dead. But he wouldn't back down. By not mobilizing all the packs, the Lycan council had allowed these damned rogues too much power already. The time had come to take back the woods. Maybe his death would serve as a wake-up call to the council that their raids on only the rogue packs who brought attention to themselves by killing humans needed to expand to include all rogues. Worry about their attitude, though, would end up someone else's problem. Lone wolves didn't get a say.

Enough stalling. Nathan drew in a breath and called out, "I'm here, you rogue bastard. Come on and show yourself. I can smell you and your lackeys."

Silence hung over the forest, an unnatural stillness that quieted even the insects that called the night their own.

"Don't tell me you're afraid to face me? Is it only women you feel capable of attacking? Coward." Nathan imbued his disgust and disdain into that one word, a gauntlet slapped down that demanded redress.

With the barest whisper of sound, from the shadows stepped a half-dozen forms. Naked forms, their skin dirty. Feral gazes lit the darkness with a reddish glow. darkness. Nathan didn't allow unease to touch him, even as the evil and unnatural glow of their eyes freaked him a bit.

As a shape stepped forward, a stench hit him, one he recognized from when he'd rescued Dana. Nathan's lip pulled back in a sneer as he beheld the pockmarked visage of the rogue leader. "If it isn't the weakling who preys on women himself."

The rogue snarled. "You're just jealous I enjoyed her first."

Nathan shook his head. "Are you really going to fuck with me? You went after *my* woman. You fucked with someone I care about. And now, I'm going to punish that rabid you going to submit to your punishment like a wolf, or force me to put you down like a rabid dog?"

As he uttered a scream of rage, the rogue's skin burst open, his limbs contorted, and his wolf bounded forth. Nathan coldly watched and called forth his beast, his half shift that gave him the cunning of man but the strength and deadliness of his wolf. He embraced the pain of his changing. He ran forward and crashed into the rogue leader. They hit the ground rolling. Nathan wrapped his hairy arm around the wolf's neck and used his sharp incisors to tear at its jugular. The hot spray and taste of blood incited the bloodfever, a good thing because the rogue's compatriots had shifted and joined in on the fun.

Nathan fought like a wild animal, his rage finally finding a release. And he used it well.

The leader managed to twist out of Nathan's grasp and slunk away on his belly, his blood still spraying in an arc from the grievous wound Nathan had given him.

Not that Nathan really noticed, caught up in a battle for survival. Snarls rang along with yelps. The scent of carnage filled the air with copper. The miasma hung in the air and coated him in a bloody mist. As body after body slumped in death or unconsciousness, Nathan began to believe he might just survive. He renewed his efforts.

A chill breeze invaded the clearing, and at its ghostly touch, the remaining wolves whimpered and backed away from Nathan until he stood alone. Nathan stood on the blood-matted grass with his chest heaving, wondering at their retreat. He growled at them to return and thumped his chest to antagonize them.

The rogue leader, still slumped on the ground, shifted back to his human shape and lay there gasping as his life force continued to seep. He managed a wet chuckle, though. "The master comes. Now you're fucked."

Nathan frowned. *Who is he talking about?*

Icy tendrils wrapped around him, ghostly fingers that made him shiver. Nathan whirled, seeking the source of his unease in the shadows, but saw nothing.

The mental barrage, when it hit, threw him to his knees, clutching his head. Like hundreds of needles piercing his brain, the agony was unbelievable. Nathan yelled at the pain and lost his grip on his beast, reverting back to his man shape. The shards of agony receded after an eternity, and he panted as he knelt.

"Figures you'd be the one who destroyed my minions."

The voice, cold and chilling, made Nathan shudder, but worse was the feeling he knew the speaker. Not one to cave to fear, he forced his gaze up to see . . . death. Not death as in the Grim Reaper himself. Not death as in a killing blow. Death in the form of a walking corpse, an impossible abomination. His father.

"Dad?" Nathan whispered the word, his mind refusing to believe the face of the man leering above him with the red eyes was the man who'd created and raised him.

A familiar brow arched, along with the sarcastic smile Nathan knew only too well. "Surprise, son!"

"But-but you're supposed to be dead," he stammered.

Nathan's father, Roderick, held out his arms expansively. "As you can see, hear, and smell, that's not exactly true."

"Impossible—"

The foot to his face caught Nathan by surprise, and he fell back. Legs encased in jeans straddled him, and his father laughed as he stared down at him. "Not impossible. Not if you're a vampire."

The wild claim saw Nathan's brow crease. "Vampires aren't real." Not real and yet look at his father. He didn't look so dead, but he also didn't look all that alive either.

What happened to him? The shock of his reappearance caused him to hesitate instead of acting.

A low chuckle left Roderick. "Not so long ago, I used to think the same thing. I mean, vampires. It's as crazy as werewolves." The genial smile never reached his eyes. "But it's true. Vampires exist. As do other things. It seems the Lycan council has hidden a lot from the packs."

Nathan slowly moved to a sitting position, body poised to act and yet, he didn't. There was so much still he didn't understand. "How did you escape the council's custody and end up a vampire?"

Roderick's brows arched in surprise. "Escape? Who said anything about that? The Lycan council owed the vampire coven, their queen, to be exact, for accidentally killing one of her handmaidens. And who better to offer up in sacrifice than a man slated for death?"

The shocking accusation made Nathan shake his head. "No, they wouldn't do that. They wouldn't give one of us up to become a monster."

"Nathan, Nathan, Nathan. How naïve of you." His father shook his head, the mockery on his face telling Nathan, without words, that he spoke true. "Of course, the council never expected the vampire queen would actually manage to turn me. It was previously considered impossible, although the queen kept trying. It was she who was originally behind the Lycan abductions and killings. She found a way to glamour the weak-minded wolves to do her bidding. But what she really wanted was a dead wolf of her own. She finally succeeded with me. And while I will admit it was beyond any horror you can imagine, the end result was quite worth it."

"What happened after she changed you?" Nathan asked, horrified yet fascinated in spite of himself at the macabre tale.

"Why, I killed her, of course. Stupid bitch, she thought she could treat me like a pet. Unfortunately, my ripping her into little pieces didn't go over well with the other vampires and placed quite the price on my head. So now I am mustering an army, one to destroy the vampires who think to keep me away from the throne that is rightfully mine."

Nathan gaped at his dead father in disbelief. "You're mad."

"Damned straight I'm pissed," his father replied, misconstruing his words. "And because of you, I keep having to rebuild my forces."

Nathan grinned, a feral smile of triumph. "It would seem your mind-controlled rogues are no match for a true alpha and his pack. Is that why you lurk in the shadows?"

Nathan was ready for the foot that came flying his way and managed to turn his head to absorb the blow. He used that moment to shift back into his beast—half-man, half-wolf—and he lunged at his father, only to find his limbs frozen.

"Ingrate. It's not enough you take my pack and send me to my death. You keep eliminating my pawns. I won't have it," Roderick roared. "I might not be able to manipulate the minds of the strong ones or enter the compound uninvited, but you are my son. My blood runs in your veins. You are tied to me, and as such, you will *obey.*"

The needles returned, and while Nathan couldn't control his limbs, his voice was free, and he screamed with the pain of it.

"Stop it!" Dana's shrill cry made his heart stop, but it was his father's evil chuckle and not the agony of his head that made the tears flow.

Chapter Seventeen

It didn't take long for John and Kody to assemble the wolves in the pack to search. Nathan hadn't taken a vehicle, which meant they could track him. They set out on foot to search for his trail. Well, Dana was on foot. The rest of the males adopted their wolf shapes. Dana trusted them to smell anything before it attacked. She had a different plan in mind.

Nathan had tried to obscure his trail, and the wolves they'd brought along split into groups of four to follow the false leads. Dana trusted her instincts—and a tugging on her heart. She ended up leading John and Kody. Her pace through the dark forest increased as certainty of Nathan's location blossomed in her mind.

Approaching the clearing where her whole life had changed, she slowed, not because of the voices she could hear but because of the sense of wrongness—*evil*—permeating the air.

She walked carefully, lest she give away her presence, all the while straining to hear the conversation. What she did hear made the tears roll down her face.

Oh, Nathan, she thought, her heart joining his in agony, an agony that increased with Nathan's screams of pain.

Regardless of her wolf mates, who nudged her to stay back, she couldn't stop herself from rushing into the clearing and crying out, "Stop it!" She had to, for Nathan's cries of pain begged an answer. Begged she save him.

Roderick, her old alpha and Nathan's dad, chuckled. The slimy sound sent a shiver skating down her spine, and she sucked in a horrified breath as she got the full impact of the monster he'd become. Once Roderick domineered via body mass and presence. He still had size, but he'd changed in other ways starting with his sunken eyes that glowed an eerie red. His canines extended past his lips in a grotesque parody of a vampire.

"Ah, the little bitch has returned. I was most disappointed when you escaped my pets. I'd hoped to use your womb to birth a new generation of pups to serve me."

"Never, you sick bastard. You leave me and Nathan alone."

Dana must have caught some kind of insanity because she faced the monster with her spine straight. It helped that Kody and John stood on either side, their muscled wolves' bodies pressed up against her. She wouldn't allow this part of her past to make her run again.

"Brave words. I wonder if you'd change your mind if you were alone."

John and Kody began howling, their bodies contorting in pain, a symphony to join that of Nathan's renewed screams.

Roderick leered. "Last time, I trusted my lackeys to handle you. This time, I think I'll stick around and make sure they don't fuck up. And speaking of birthing the next generation, why don't we start right now? I'll even be nice and let my dear son do the honors first. Of course, he won't be the one in the driver's seat for his body. I will."

Dana shuddered as his words penetrated. But the true horror was seeing Nathan's body twitch and then stand, his movements jerky like that of a marionette. He approached her on stilted legs, his eyes open wide in horror.

"No," he moaned. "Run, Dana."

She read the plea in his eyes. She also saw his love for her as he fought his father's control. Flight was the easy path. She had taken that route before and left Nathan to face the pain alone. She wouldn't do it again.

"Hey Roderick, anyone ever tell you that you suck as a dad?" Dana, who'd worn clothes for a reason, whipped out her pistol and with an aim practiced over years, shot the vamp between the eyes.

Roderick fell back, a bullet hole in his forehead and a surprised look on his face. He fell to the ground and didn't get back up.

For a moment, everyone was still. Everyone watched.

The body didn't move. An almost collective sigh of relief went through them. He was dead. Truly dead.

The frozen moment of uncertainty shattered and Dana found herself suddenly surrounded by male bodies—naked ones.

"Damn it, woman! What were you thinking?" John yelled as he hugged her.

"Hot damn, you gotta give me lessons," Kody exclaimed with clear admiration.

Dana pushed them aside to see where Nathan was and saw him still standing a few feet away, a look of uncertainty on his face. She walked to him and opened her arms.

When he still didn't move, she put her hands on her hips. "Get your ass over here right now, mister. As my mate, I expect a hug after I shoot really freaky bad guys."

His lips twitched, but he stopped fighting himself. He swept her into his arms and hugged her so tight she squeaked.

She hugged him back and whispered, "Caught you."

* * * *

Nathan held Dana and marveled that, after everything that had happened, she still wanted him. She'd saved him, not just from his monster of a father but himself.

Nathan set her down and, when John cautiously approached, dragged him in close for a hug, a quick one. They were naked, after all. "Thanks for coming, brother," he whispered.

Kody had no problem with a naked hug, and he tackled the two of them in his enthusiasm. "Woo! The terrible trio back in action again."

It was only when they realized that Dana watched their naked huddle with twinkling eyes and a smirk that they broke apart with a lot of throat clearing and back thumping.

"Um, guys, where did Roderick go?" Dana's hesitant words made them all whirl and peer, only to see that not only had Roderick disappeared, but the rogues had slunk off too. The question she wondered was did Roderick get up on his own, or did the rogues carry off their leader?

The rest of the pack took that moment to show up, and Nathan barked out some orders to the wolves, mostly asking what they'd seen. But none of them saw anything. No one scented anything. It seemed impossible, just like his father's very existence. Who knows what tricks Roderick had. He sent the freshly arrived pack members in groups to fan out and maybe catch those fleeing.

He prepared to follow when Dana's

smaller hand slipped into his. She peered up at him. "Don't go."

"I should. He's my father."

"He's a monster. And there's no way he survived a bullet to the head."

"Why would the rogues take his body if he was dead?"

"Why do those bastards do anything?" She gripped his shirt and pulled him close. "Let it go, Nathan. You almost died once already tonight. I don't think I could lose you again. I need you."

"You need all of us," he corrected including his pack mates. "But my Pack also need a leader right now which is why I have to go look for Roderick."

Except Roderick and the rogues were nowhere to be found. They'd vanished as if into thin air and that ominous press against the mind didn't return.

He sent his pack off to bed, and rejoined Dana who'd refused to leave until she knew Nathan and the others were safe.

He shifted and dropped to his knees before her. "They escaped."

"They might have but you won today. The whole pack won. You fought off Roderick and his gang."

"But they might return."

"And if they do…"

"Then I'll kill him." No hesitation next

time.

"Oh Nathan." She reached down and cupped his cheek. The gentle gesture didn't go unnoticed by his pack mates. Her mates. Now his brothers for life.

He stood and gripped her hand. "I think it's time."

"Are you sure?" she asked, peering up at him with concern.

More than sure. "For so long I let myself be worried about losing you to someone else. I let my jealousy push you away. No more. I need to do this, show you and my mating brothers that we're a family pack now. I can't think of a better way than by making love to you, for all of us to love you if you're up to it. Or was I mistaken in thinking you wanted to experiment with a ménage?"

"If you think you're ready, then I think I'd enjoy that very much. Boys?" She turned a questioning look to John and Kody, who grinned. The tantalizing scent of Dana's arousal drifted up, and Nathan's cock rose. "Last one to the house comes last," she taunted as she sprinted off into the woods.

With a look sideways to the men he'd share the rest of his life with, he shrugged and laughed. "Just remember to keep your dicks to yourself."

A moment later, he and his shifted brothers bounded off into the woods after their mate, following the trail of clothing she left and her she-wolf scent.

She led them on a merry chase, but they knew these woods. Nathan burst into the house first, followed by John and Kody. They moved into the house, sniffing the air in an attempt to find her, when they heard a giggle from behind.

"Oh, dear, I guess I'm last. What a shame for me," Dana said, sauntering in, naked and proud. Then she wrinkled her nose. "Okay, I'm sorry, but first we all need a shower because the reek of evil just isn't attractive."

Nathan hardened further at the sight of her happy smile. Suddenly impatient to get to the main event, he scooped her up and threw her over his shoulder. "Come on, boys. I've got the largest shower and bed. I think it's time we taught our mate here just who's in charge."

Dana squealed. "Hey, what do you think you're doing?"

John reached a hand over and tweaked her nipple. "Preparing to make you come last."

Kody chuckled. "Hot damn, this is gonna be fun."

Nathan slid a hand up to sit between her thighs, the heat from her core radiating hot enough to stir his lust. He gave her sex a quick stroke and felt her shuddering response. "I call dibs on her ass."

"My what?" she exclaimed.

"Mouth," Kody chimed in.

"What a chore. I get her pussy," John said, an evident grin in his tone.

Reaching his bathroom, Nathan swung her down to cradle her in his arms as John adjusted the temperature. He caught her lips in a kiss that set him on fire and wondered if perhaps he should have opted for her luscious mouth. But the thought of her tight ass gripping him made him shudder.

He stepped into the shower, glad he'd splurged on a large walk-in stall version. Although with three large men and one smaller woman, the space still ended up tight. He knew some of the body parts brushing his, skin to skin, didn't belong to Dana, but he forgave that minor weirdness at the languorous look in Dana's eyes. She looked drunk on bliss already.

John and Kody rinsed off quickly and left to prepare the bed. Alone with Dana, Nathan clasped her tight to him, his erection throbbing against her belly.

She licked her lips and gazed up at him. "I love you, Nathan. You don't have to do this if you're not ready."

Nathan chuckled as he traced her full lower lip with a finger. "Oh, I'm ready. The question is, are you afraid of me taking your ass?"

Her eyes glazed, and she swayed into him. "Yes. No. I know you won't hurt me."

"Never again," he whispered as he leaned

down to kiss her.

Afraid he'd do her up against the wall before he'd proven himself to her, he grabbed the soap and rubbed himself. He didn't say a word when she stole the soap from him and washed his back, her hands lingering over his buttocks. She pressed herself against his back, her pebbled nipples poking into him as her arms reached around. Her soapy hands grabbed hold of him and stroked his jutting cock, and Nathan sucked in a breath.

Good as it felt, though, he wanted more. He wanted to sink his shaft inside of her, feel her clench around him as she came.

He turned. Breaking her grip and holding her at arm's length, he rinsed them. They emerged to find towels being offered by his mating brothers. Nathan dried himself but watched with glittering eyes as Kody and John shared the task of drying Dana. Their hands lingered on her body, tweaking a nipple here, stroking across her cleft there.

Nathan waited for his enemy, jealousy, to rouse and breathed a sigh of relief when all he felt was arousal. They led her to the bedroom and the bed, stripped of its comforter and pillows, a cleared area ready for the main event.

Without words, they laid her down and crawled onto the bed, John and Kody each to a side, while Nathan got the spot between her legs.

Then they went to work, playing with her body, preparing her for their cocks.

* * * *

Dana basked in the attention they laved on her. What a change. She'd gone from playing alone with herself to having three men—*my mates*—determined to please her.

Kody and John had each laid claim to a breast, but while they both tortured her, their technique differed, from the way John liked to swirl his tongue around her areola to Kody, who liked to nibble. She would have arched at their touch had they not held her down. She craned to find Nathan, suddenly fearing he'd left, unable to handle the situation. But she found him, kneeling between her legs, stroking his cock.

He caught her perusal and smiled, a slow, sensuous thing that made her quiver at the promise in it.

He let go of his rod and bent forward, his mouth hovering over her sex. Dana moaned as he blew on it. He cupped her buttocks and lifted her up. She clenched tight, waiting for his touch, but when it came, it wasn't where she expected. He licked her anus, his wet tongue sliding across her rosette an odd sensation.

She both feared and anticipated his claim that he would take her ass. She knew women did it, but in her inexperience, she'd never imagined she'd be one of them. But as he probed that tight ring with his tongue, that, along with all the other touches to her body, made her relax. After everything that had happened, it seemed only fitting that Nathan got to be first to claim that virgin hole.

His mouth slid away and covered her sex. Dana moaned loudly at the hot feel then gasped as he poked a finger at her rosette.

"Relax," he murmured against her mound.

Kody and John redoubled their efforts on her breasts and distracted her enough that Nathan pushed his finger in. She tightened again at the strange sensation. Nathan bit down lightly on her clit. Dana tried to thrash, but pinned, she could only tremble, the sheer pleasure overriding the strange sensation of her ass being penetrated.

"Push out against his finger," Kody coaxed, his lips wandering to the shell of her ear.

Dana did as told and found the pressure lessened. Nathan pushed a second finger in, and she concentrated on pushing out, a concentration lost when Nathan began eating her pussy in earnest. His lips tugged and sucked on her sex then probed it to lap at her.

Dana found herself thrusting her hips against his mouth and only belatedly realized her arching was in rhythm with his fingers thrusting in her ass. She also noticed that the sensation had veered from uncomfortable to strangely enjoyable. There was movement on the bed as bodies shuffled position, and she lost a mouth on her breast as a new finger penetrated her. She opened eyes, heavy with desire, to see John had joined Nathan, his fingers replacing Nathan's in her ass and then adding one more. Nathan moved until he lay beside Dana. He pulled her face close for a kiss, and she sucked in his tongue.

Kody lifted her and laid her atop Nathan facing away while John's fingers kept working her anus. John removed his fingers from her and bent his mouth to lap at her cunt. The wide head of Nathan's cock probed at her rosette, and she felt a moment's apprehension. It was so much larger than the fingers. But John kept lapping at her pussy while Nathan crooned words of love and encouragement in her ear.

The head of his cock popped past her tight ring, and she cried out at the pressure and stretching sensation. Kody muffled her cry by sliding the head of his own shaft across her lips.

"Suck me," he ordered.

Dana needed the distraction and opened wide. Kody thrust in at the same time as Nathan pumped his hips up and seated his cock fully into her ass. Dana screamed around the rod in her mouth, not from pain but from the fullness of it.

John bit down on her clit again and sent a spasm through her channel. She shook from all the sensations then truly quivered when John began to push his cock into her pussy.

Surely it wouldn't fit, but to her surprise and pleasure, it did. Her orgasm hit before they even started moving. It refused to hold off with so much going on. She wailed around Kody's cock as he pumped her mouth. Then she screamed some more as Nathan and John started to thrust. In and out, they alternated sheathing themselves in her. Her body quivered, the muscles in her pelvis squeezing tight.

"Holy fuck," she heard John grunt a moment before he spurted hotly inside her.

He withdrew his cock from her sex while Nathan kept thrusting, and Dana almost mourned its loss. Kody pulled out from her mouth, and a moment later he positioned himself between her legs. His large size made Nathan grunt under her, especially when Kody thrust in time with Nathan, the pair of them seating themselves fully at the same time. In and out, their dual steel rods pummeled her flesh, and Dana rode the blissful crest of their lovemaking while another lover held her body down, lest she fall off Nathan.

With the next orgasm, Dana literally saw stars so deeply did the waves of bliss rack her body. Her whole body pulsed with it. Within seconds Nathan and Kody each yelled as they found their own release inside her.

Sweaty, sticky, but sated, so deliciously sated, Dana found herself sandwiched in a sea of bodies.

She sighed, happier than she'd ever been.

"Are you okay?" John asked in concern.

"Mmm-hmm," was all she could utter.

"Hot damn, she's speechless," Kody crowed.

"And all it took was a massive orgy," Nathan added dryly.

Dana giggled. "I do not talk that much."

"Really?" The skepticism in their voices made her laugh again.

"Well, I guess you guys don't want to hear me say just how much I love you all then."

Bodies went rolling, and Dana found herself on her back with John leaning over her. "I love you, Dana. Even if you do snore."

"I do—" Her rebuttal was muffled by John's lips. When he let her up for air, she smiled at him softly. "I love you, John. You're my rock."

A shove sent John flying, and Kody clambered over her next, his green eyes dancing. "Darling, I absolutely love you. So do you think I can get your ass next time?" He waggled his brows hopefully, and Dana choked.

"Um, while I love you dearly and you make me laugh, I don't think my poor ass could take that kind of abuse yet."

She pursed her lips for a kiss, and Kody dove in for a smooch—and added some tongue.

She was slightly breathless when he was manhandled aside and Nathan took his place. His blue eyes peered down at her with such love that tears pricked her eyes.

"I promise to never run again," she whispered. "I love you, Nathan."

"I promise to never give you a reason to," he murmured back, his voice thick. "I love you, Dana. And the next time you decide to defy pack law, I vow to stay by your side."

Then he kissed her, and Dana closed her eyes as the emotional ties that bound them came full circle.

No matter what the future holds, I'll face it because I am no longer alone.

Epilogue

Dana lay in a tangle of limbs that made her smile. How she'd made the jump from no mate to three, all at once, still baffled her at times, but she thanked her stars she'd come to her senses.

It had been almost a month since the showdown with Nathan's dad, and while rogue activity had dropped, they were still constantly on guard. Dana had also taken to carrying a stake around along with her handy-dandy pistol.

Nathan had confronted the Lycan council with the fact of his father's state of being, and things had turned ugly. For the council, that was. A number of packs backed him when Nathan asked for the entire council's removal and a trial for their misdoings, not that the cocky council members were admitting to anything. In the meantime, Nathan, along with some other pack leaders, had taken over interim leadership of the council. He'd already confided to her that if the post became permanent, the first thing he'd do was make changes to the pack laws to give women more rights and the ability to make their own choices.

He'd earned himself a BJ for that. And apparently she'd done it well enough for him to gasp, as his eyes rolled back in his head, to let him know if there were any other laws he could abolish for her.

Life truly had changed for the better. Twelve years ago, when she'd defied pack law, she'd thought she'd never find happiness again, that she was destined to wander through life alone. It turned out that her running away was the best decision she'd ever made, regardless of the bumps along that road. She still had a defiant side, but nowadays, she preferred to use it to her advantage. How could she not when her mates loved to throw her over their shoulders and punish her in delightfully wicked ways?

Of course, they'd probably have to stop the over-the-shoulder caveman carry for a bit. With the surprise in her tummy, she could just imagine how overprotective they'd all become.

As the bodies around her roused and hands began to grope at her, she smiled. *Screw the love of one man. I'll take three any day.*

The End

For more of the Pack, please see the other books in the series: Defying Pack Law, Betraying the Pack, Seeking Pack Redemption, New Pack Order
More books at EveLanglais.com

CPSIA information can be obtained
at www.ICGtesting.com
Printed in the USA
FFOW02n2046120417
34546FF